D0375872

Girls Lost

Jessica Schiefauer

Translated from the Swedish by Saskia Vogel

NO LONGER PROPERTY OF
SEATTLE PUBLIC LIBRARY

Deep Vellum Publishing
Dallas, Texas

Deep Vellum Publishing
3000 Commerce St., Dallas, Texas 75226
deepvellum.org · @deepvellum

Deep Vellum is a 501c3 nonprofit literary arts organization
founded in 2013 with the mission to bring
the world into conversation through literature.

Copyright © Jessica Schiefauer, 2011
Published by agreement with the Hedlund Agency
English translation copyright © Saskia Vogel, 2020
First published in Sweden as *Pojkarna* by Bonnier Carlsen in 2011.
First edition, 2020.
All rights reserved.

Support for this publication has been provided in part by grants from the
National Endowment for the Arts, the Texas Commission on the Arts, the City of Dallas
Office of Arts and Culture's ArtsActivate program, and the Moody Fund for the Arts:

The cost of this translation was defrayed by a subsidy from the
Swedish Arts Council, gratefully acknowledged.

**SWEDISH
ARTS COUNCIL**

ISBNs: 9781941920954 (paperback) | 9781941920961 (ebook)

LIBRARY OF CONGRESS CATALOGING-IN-PUBLICATION DATA
Names: Schiefauer, Jessica, author. | Vogel, Saskia, translator.
Title: Girls lost / Jessica Schiefauer ; translated from the Swedish by
    Saskia Vogel.
Other titles: Pojkarna. English
Description: First edition. | Dallas, Texas : Deep Vellum Publishing, 2020.
Identifiers: LCCN 2019054713 | ISBN 9781941920954 (trade paperback) | ISBN
    9781941920961 (ebook)
Subjects: CYAC: Adolescence--Fiction. | Sexual harassment—Fiction. |
    Gender identity—Fiction. | Friendship—Fiction. | Magic—Fiction.
Classification: LCC PZ7.1.S33615 Gir 2020 | DDC [Fic]--dc23
LC record available at https://lccn.loc.gov/2019054713

Cover Design by Anna Zylicz | annazylicz.com
Interior Layout and Typesetting by Kirby Gann

Text set in Bembo, a typeface modeled on typefaces cut by Francesco Griffo for Aldo
Manuzio's printing of *De Aetna* in 1495 in Venice

Printed in the United States of America

This is a work of fiction. Names, characters, places, and incidents either are the product of
the author's imagination or are used fictitiously, and any resemblance to actual persons, living
or dead, businesses, companies, events, or locales is entirely coincidental.

*The real voyage of discovery consists not in seeking
new landscapes, but in having new eyes.*

Marcel Proust

I HAVE A STORY to tell, but my story isn't for just anyone. It's a story for those who want to see, for those who dare lift a magnifying glass to their eye and contemplate the wonder. If you are blind to such things, then this story isn't for you; but if your eyes are open, listen carefully.

It begins in a glade one spring evening as the spruce trees' trunks glow red. The sky is twilight blue, the forest quiet and still, and through the thin windowpanes of the old house comes the telephone's shrill, summoning ring.

I STOP DEAD in my tracks, astounded by the echo of the sudden noise.

On the table, the house phone is a mute beast, a black old-fashioned thing that hasn't made a sound as long as I've lived here. But now it's jingling, jangling, hoarse as an old dog. I toss the weeds aside, warily approach the house, and press down on the door handle. The door glides open and I cross the wooden floor; the forest's evening perfume follows me in. Wet with soil, my fingers grip the clunky receiver, the signal buzzes in my palm. Slowly I raise it to my ear, listen. The storm of breath in the mouthpiece betrays me.

"Kim? Is that you?"

The voice has aged but I know it well, and I grip the receiver with both hands, squeezing it with my dirty fingers. If my vocal cords weren't rusty from lack of use I'd be screaming, out of dread and for joy at once. When I open my mouth the words barely manage to escape:

"Yes. It's me."

"At last. I've been looking all over!"

I shut my eyes. Her face appears, one of her faces: fourteen years old and freckled, a natural blush to her cheeks. My mouth is dry, I collect saliva and try to come up with something to say, can't find anything but:

"It's been a long time."

"Yeah, it has. It really has."

BELLA, THE PIGEON-TOED girl, who was always on the verge of stuttering and blushing and being tongue-tied at school.

Bella, who planted a shoot in the black earth and gave me life.

We lived in the same neighborhood of townhouses, I could see her house from my window. With my eyes shut, the memory is clear: Bella and the games and the greenhouse that was like a small palace beyond the garden hedge.

Bella cultivated flowers. She had her own greenhouse—not a mini one for children, a real full-size one. She tended to everything herself: the greenhouse and the garden. In Bella's house there was no parent who cooked or cleaned, no one who responded to notices of parent-teacher conferences or invitations to Christmas plays and graduations. There was a father, he took strong pills and spent his days in a haze. There was no mother around. Bella would tell people that her mother had died in childbirth. To me she said nothing at all, but there were stories, chitter and chatter crept around the houses, dribbling into our child-ears even though we weren't meant to hear. The mental hospital, said the chitter, ran away with another woman, said the chatter. But no one knew for sure.

Bella's grandmother gave her the greenhouse. I have a distant memory of her: she was red-headed, like Bella, and when she smiled her red gums were vivid in contrast to her pale skin. She arrived with her cases and bags when Bella was still small, moved into one of the townhouse's bare rooms, dug up a patch of earth in the derelict garden, and started cultivating it. As soon as Bella was old enough her grandmother showed her how to plant seeds, how to cull and weed. Then one day the grandmother disappeared too. Her things were gone; in the room where she had lived nothing but a compact mirror was left and a long, red strand of hair that wrapped itself around

Bella's finger when she picked it up. But on their garden plot was a newly built greenhouse with leaded windows that flashed in the sunshine, and from that day on Bella spent all her free time in there. Her enthusiasm knew no bounds, nothing in the world of plants was too insignificant to be investigated. She took impeccable care of the flowers, pruning them and feeding them so that they, their colors and shapes, could thrive and radiate. In the entire neighborhood, no other garden was as vibrant as hers.

I'M STANDING THERE, receiver in hand, gaze fixed on the twilight outside, the evening blue washing away my memories.

"What do you want?"

Bella exhales, the air rumbles in the receiver.

"I want you to come back."

A shiver runs down my spine. I bite my lip, my voice is barely a whisper.

"I don't know."

Bella doesn't answer at first. Then she says, slowly:

"Kim, you have to. You owe us that much. Momo is already on her way."

She hangs up with a ding. I'm still holding the receiver. The emptiness buzzes in my ear. I want to hear more of Bella's voice, so recently present, but already gone.

MOMO'S HAIR WAS a dark brown cascade, she stood tall and had a curious gaze, and one day she'd simply appeared in front of us on the sidewalk in the neighborhood. She had a question, we had an answer, and after that we were inseparable. A bundle of energy she was, dragging me along to bazaars and flea markets at the edge of the city, putting weird hats on my head and hanging ugly shawls around my neck, saying, "Buy them!" And I would laugh and say, "No way, not on your life." Then Momo would smile and buy them herself, no matter how ugly they were. She was a child of artists, raised in a large house in the country warped by creativity. When they moved into our area it didn't take long for the talk to start. Her family was like none we had ever seen. Her mother had her studio in their living room and the dad had his on the top floor. He was an architect and she a seamstress; they only took on work when they had to. Mostly they sat around as if spellbound by their materials. The dad made landscapes and figures out of clay, plaster, latex, and papier-mâché. The mom collected fabrics and objects, which she transformed into creations, sometimes wearable, sometimes not. In the midst of all this they raised one daughter. She was christened Monica but to us she was Momo.

Momo knew the art of observation and notation. Everything created in her parents' home she made her own. In her hands all materials were pliable, there was nothing she couldn't knead, chisel, cut, fold, or tack. She always had some sort of project going. Her eyes sparkled when she fed the fabric between the sharp sewing machine needles and sometimes her voice went up into falsetto because she was so excited to tell us about what it would be like once it was done.

WE TURNED FOURTEEN that spring, Bella, Momo, and I.

We kept to ourselves.

In winter we were mostly in Momo's room but during the hot time of year we kept to Bella's garden, or the greenhouse when it rained. We listened to the insects and to the rain, watched the droplets on the petals evaporate when the sun broke through. Curious, we watched the flower flies mate in the oxeye daisies—a strange and violent dance that sent shivers through the thin petals. During dry spells we watered at night. Bella filled the green can over by the house and we helped carry it across the lawn. She never asked us to help but neither did she stop us, wordlessly showing us what to do. She knew the names and types of flowers but she rarely shared them and I didn't ask, it wasn't important to me. Her flowerbeds dazzled like New Year's fireworks and like all fireworks they were best at night, when the streetlights' soft yellow glow spread through the neighborhood. You might have thought the velvety leaves would close up when it was dark but they didn't. They opened up to the night, screaming at the stars:

I'm over here!

Look at me!

The night is black BUT I AM IN COLOR!

We lived amidst this sparkle and it made me forget that I was Kim, that I had a growing, bursting body. The greenhouse was a free zone, a space governed by other laws. The school days and hallways and my parents' house—everything fell away when I walked through that glass door. Even Bella became someone else in there. Her eyes were calm and sharp as a knife, her movements were precise and confident. At school she was a chubby girl with red hair and freckles, a girl who preferred to sit quietly and stay invisible for as long as possible. And me, I was a sad skinny thing with lanky legs and an oversized head. My skin flamed with eczema as soon as it came in contact with any unknown substance—I couldn't handle the hot summer sun or cold winter winds, nor could I eat red tomatoes or golden oranges. They gave me a flaming rash around my mouth and nostrils, and I would have to rub stinky ointment into my skin for days in a row. My girl-skin preferred paper-dry air and wallpapered walls, strip lighting and linoleum, and chlorinated water.

I hated it.

My body clung to me like something foreign—a sticky, itchy rubber suit; but no matter how much I scratched and scraped at it, it was where it was. At night I dreamed of shedding my body. It was so simple, suddenly a zipper appeared in my skin. Sometimes it was along my inner thigh, sometimes across my stomach, along my back or between my legs. I opened it, I could feel the air flowing toward my real skin underneath, like a vacuum seal breaking. And I peeled off my skin, climbed out of it like a soiled garment and I could feel the cool floor against my new soles. But before I could get to the mirror and discover what I actually looked like, I'd wake up.

I told Bella about this dream once, while she was culling her red flowerbed. I was crouching down next to her, handing her the spade and the hand rake, and I told her exactly how it felt—what it was like when my skin loosened and fell off me. Bella had dirt on her face, a blade of grass at her hairline, and she listened earnestly. She didn't say a word, but I knew she got me.

Yes, we turned fourteen that spring and we hid in the greenhouse to avoid growing up. We stayed away from people our own age, we were wary of heeding the call of the hormones in our blood because we suspected that they could overpower us at any time, without our consent. We knew what was waiting for us: one morning we'd simply get out of bed and know that the time for children's games was done. We'd look around, see what everyone else was doing, and do the same. Learn to drink, smoke, kiss. Learn to tolerate boys touching us. All we would have to do would be to walk straight ahead, putting one foot in front of the other until our ankle muscles were strong enough so as not to twist when we wore slender high heels.

We didn't want to, Bella, Momo, and I.

We refused!

Our bodies wailed and writhed, we itched with restlessness. We walked around like large irate animals in our parents' houses, shouting for something that could still the strange swells, but wherever we looked we all we saw were ready-made Female Models. We shut our mouths and closed our eyes, refusing to accept the inevitable. It was instinctive, an ember in the chest: anything could happen to us—just not that. So we fled to the greenhouse, turned away from the world, sought comfort in the earth and the flowers and the insects.

SCHOOL DAYS WERE MADE up of combat strategy and clashes.

People crowded in the hallways, girls with girls and boys with boys. We practiced making it look like we were completely consumed by what was happening in the group. We listened to the person talking or showing off or taking center stage in some other way; meanwhile, we kept an eye on the halls: who was coming and going, where they were walking, what their expressions were communicating. Because it could happen at any time, anyone could make a not-insignificant gesture, a not-insignificant sound with their tongue, or take a not-insignificant step in our direction.

It happened all the time. Some boys would walk past some girls and right when they were in line with each other one of the boys would stick standing close, so close their breath built a wall in front of our faces and it was impossible to turn away because they were everywhere. They licked our cheeks with the tips of their tongues, searching for our lips, their boy-hands ran up our thighs and they whispered things, rumbling false declarations of love in saccharine tones. And if you managed to keep your mouth shut the whole time, if you kept your eyes fixed on the ground as they probed you with their hands and tongues, then it would end with a shove to the chest and a loogie at your feet. Before they'd turn their backs on us, they would hiss about what disgusting, ugly cunts we were, so fucking disgusting no boy would ever want to fuck us even if he got paid to do it.

We kept our mouths shut, counted backward in our heads to keep still while waiting for it to pass. But sometimes it burst. Then we hissed back at the boys, Momo, Bella, and I. We hissed at them to leave us alone, trying to tear ourselves from their grip, spit in their faces, knee them. But they were so much stronger; hopelessly, unfairly, unbelievably stronger. All they did was laugh at us, grab his elbow to his crotch and shoot his forearm up like an erection. He'd tense his arm, squeeze his fist, mimic the sounds he'd heard in the movies he watched with other boys. Another boy would note this gesture and start stabbing his tongue at the inside of his cheek. Then they'd let out a collective howl, and a deluge of fleshy porn dialogue would be unleashed on the girls.

There was only one way to respond: keep your mouth shut and head held high; keep your mask intact even though those words and gestures always got under your skin. Mostly we weathered it. We fixed our eyes on each other and whoever was talking would forget what she was talking about, but she kept talking anyway. We encouraged her with nods, soundlessly we convinced each other that "It's okay, don't worry about them, don't turn around, keep talking, don't show them you're afraid, *for God sake don't show the you're afraid.*"

But sometimes the crowd of boys approache with something unyielding in their eyes, whe we were specially chosen and they circled u us by the wrist and smile at our tiny balled fists. It was them and only them who could decide when the game was over.

I couldn't handle it. I hated them. I could endure any and every humiliation, if only I didn't have to deal with those double-edged, backhanded signals directed at us alone, at us girls. The dripping saccharine lines, their hands nonetheless hot against our bodies, their crooked smiles that in spite of everything made something flicker in our chests, only to be tossed aside and spit on, proving just how insufficient and disgusting we were.

At night I lay awake and tried to shut my eyes to what was happening. I tried to forget their hands and their gazes and their breath and I frantically tried to figure out how to rid myself of what provoked them. I daydreamed about revenge, I was large in those dreams, large and tough and strong and my voice was deep. I bellowed at the boys and my voice made their hair blow backward, my saliva showered their cheeks. Then they ran, and I lumbered along like a giant, a hero in the hallways.

But in reality I wasn't large and tough, I was thin and lanky and there was no way to rid myself of what provoked them.

BELLA SENT OFF for plants from all over the world. At least once a month I went with her to the post office to pick up a package. She'd carry it home, eyes twinkling, then spent hours sorting the contents at the kitchen table. The seeds were packed in opaque paper envelopes from which unusual smells escaped once you opened them. A few were large as walnuts and others were like white grains of sand, you could hardly tell there was anything in those envelopes at all. In some packages were large lumps with shoots and air roots, and others were small perforated plastic cubes filled with earth from which grew a dainty pale green sprout.

Bella delighted in her purchases. She kept her large botany book open and I helped her check the text on the packages against the invoice. Bella ran her finger along the book's table of contents, sounding out the flower's Latin name as she searched: *Miltonia candida, Oncidium tigrinum, Vanilla planifolia.* Then we compared the picture of the flower with the picture on the package, so Bella would know for sure what would be growing in her beds.

One Saturday morning we were sitting with a fresh package in Bella's kitchen. We were done, everything was accounted for. Bella nodded in satisfaction, she was just about to repack the shipment, when she caught sight of something.

"There's more."

In the box was a little plastic bottle and at its bottom was a small green lump. From the lump sprouted a thin, green leaf. Bella held the bottle up to the lamp, turning it gently. I craned my neck, squinting into the light.

"What is it?"

Bella frowned, examining it.

"Some sort of shoot. Maybe an orchid?"

She turned the bottle over, looking for some text, but it was blank. We checked the invoice again but there weren't any additional items. Bella shrugged and left her chair.

"We'll plant it in the greenhouse. And see what happens."

THE NEXT MORNING Bella was at our front door, holding down the doorbell with her thumb, and knocking for good measure. Upstairs, my parents muttered and wondered what was going on, it was Sunday morning after all, for God's sake, but I slipped on a pair of sweatpants, tiptoed out into the hall and opened the door. Bella tumbled over the threshold, grabbing me by the shoulders.

"It's fantastic, it's *truly fantastic*!"

She turned around and ran straight onto the street, off toward her house. She didn't look around, didn't wait. Bleary-eyed, I leaned against the doorframe, looking for something to put on my feet.

That morning I was in Bella's garden, wearing only a nightgown and Dad's rain boots. The spring wind permeated the thin fabric. I looked in through the low doorway and there she was.

There she was!

Just a stalk, so far. A gangly pale green stalk, half a meter tall, topped with a drop-shaped bud, ready to burst.

Bella's arm grazed mine, her skin was cold and goose pimpled. Her voice was trembling.

"All in one day, Kim. One day!"

I looked the stalk up and down. It was probably soft to the touch.

"When do you think it will bloom?"

"Any minute now! It won't be long."

She shook her fluffy red head, bit her lip thoughtfully.

"No, it really won't be much longer."

I practically had to drag Bella out of there. She would have preferred to have her breakfast in the greenhouse. She thought we should bring our *fil* milk and cereal and jam in there and watch over the plant night and day, skipping school and then carrying out our sleeping bags and sleeping mats and flashlights. But I refused. It was too cold for that; it was only April, even the snowdrops had barely come out of hibernation.

ONE RAINY, WINDY afternoon, the three of us cuddled up in Momo's bed and flipped through strange magazines. Momo had stolen them from her parents' locked desk drawer and the covers were stamped with the word IMPORT in large black letters. They were catalogs of some sort, but the models were almost naked and wearing animal masks. I thought it was creepy but Momo's eyes glinted along with the glossy pages. She ran her tongue over her lips, stroked her finger over the masked faces, traced the tiger's painted whiskers with her fingernail. Then she slapped the magazine shut.

"A masquerade! We have to have a masquerade, right?"

She hopped off the bed, opened the lid of the wooden trunk where she kept her fabrics.

"With costumes and masks, I'll sew them! And food! And dancing!"

Her cheeks were red. There was something enticing about the word—*masquerade*—it sounded foreign and colorful. A new reflection in the mirror, a costume, a mask to glue on top of Kim, the quiet ratty-haired chapped-skin one, Kim, the pale earnest fragile one.

I never talked about it, but sometimes I was so jealous of Momo and Bella. They had their interests; I had nothing. If it wasn't for them, I'd have nothing but that large void I carried, the feeling that something deep down inside me was out of whack.

I nodded eagerly.

"Yes, let's do it, let's do it! Can we, Bella, please?"

And now the two of us were looking at Bella, like we were trying to snare her in our joy. Sometimes she would scoff and call Momo's ideas "fancies," and each time I thought it was her grandmother talking. But now she was smiling her thoughtful smile and nodding along.

"We can use the greenhouse."

She looked at the carpet for a second.

"I mean, Dad'll be home, but you know how he is."

Of course we did, but her garden was the most beautiful place I knew. Excitement rose through my body, and I clapped with delight.

"Yes, yes, yes! Tonight!"

But Momo dismissed me with a wave of her index finger, then rooted around in the chest and took out a measuring tape.

"You know we can't, it's still too cold, and there's so much to do! Come here, arms out, let me measure."

Bella and I got up. For a long time we stood in our socks with our arms stretched out like airplane wings while she wrapped the measuring tape around us and made notes in her notebook. I glanced at Bella. The light in her eyes was the same as the light in mine.

That very night came a knock on my window. The two of them were standing outside. Momo was sleepy and tousled but Bella was wide awake. I swept the blanket over my pajamas, climbed out through the window and shivered when my bare feet met the wet grass.

The wind had eased, the night was deep blue and redolent and the table outside the greenhouse was piled with books. Bella had dragged her entire botanical library out before waking us up. Now the three of us were standing there, amazed and shivering, her eyes open wide.

She rose like a queen under that glass roof. Her head was large and trumpet-shaped. It looked heavy and moist but it wasn't bowed toward the stalk, it was sturdy and held high and seemed to be looking up at the night sky. Her face made me think of thirst and longing and open mouths: dark-violet leaf tongues surrounding something tender, pale, and yellow deep inside. The school nurse's voice ran through my head, talking about how pubic hair grows in puberty to protect the newly developed sex organ. I shook my head to get rid of that voice. It felt ugly thinking about something like that in the presence of her.

Momo's arms were crossed and she was staring, her voice was sleepy.

"What is it?"

Bella smiled and cocked her head, her expression revealed nothing but wise wonder. Under her nails were dark lines of earth and her knees were grass green in the bright night. Without a word, she took Momo's wrist. Momo didn't protest, she let Bella guide her hand to the flower's head. Bella showed her how to touch the petals, tickle her with her fingertips. And then we saw it, all three of us.

She seemed to sigh, leaning her large head into Momo's hand, letting herself be scratched.

Momo was breathless. She pulled her hand back very slowly and a few seconds passed before she whispered:

"How did it do that?"

Bella caressed the velvety underside of the leaves.

"I think she's a carnivore. A meat-eater. They feel something when you touch them and if it's worth the trouble they catch it, dissolve it and suck it into themselves."

Momo held her own hand, disgusted, and I felt a little ashamed, because for a second I really did think the flower was magical. Of course I'd heard of meat-eating flowers, but I'd never seen one. I didn't think they could be so... beautiful.

Bella didn't see us, she only had eyes for the flower.

"I *think* she's a carnivore. But I can't find her in any of my books."

FINALLY THE HEAT arrived, and with it the evening of our first masquerade.

We were as rowdy as small children before an evening at the circus. We'd spent the week running back and forth between the townhouses, breathlessly watching as our costumes grew out of Momo's magical hands. Momo and I'd gotten permission to sleep over at Bella's. Momo's parents had agreed right away and mine hadn't said no either, even if they were a bit surprised by what I told them we were going to do. My mother just nodded when I asked, but I saw her worried eyes flit across my new womanly shapes, across my face that had begun to wear a new expression in these past months. When she thought I couldn't hear her, she talked in a hushed voice with Dad about it, cautiously suggesting that we might be getting a bit too old for this stuff, wasn't it time to leave these childish dress-up games behind. But Dad just chuckled. "Count yourself lucky that she still prefers these childish games," he said. "The time will come when she won't and it will get worse." When our special day finally arrived, I left my parents' tidy house at twilight, nightgown and toothbrush in my backpack.

Bella had dragged the garden furniture out to the lawn by the greenhouse and surrounded it with burning candles. On the rickety table was a tray with the brown teapot, cups, the honey jar, and a large bowl of cookies and fruit. Bella was in charge of her dad's ATM card. She was usually the one who made sure that there was food at home and her dad never asked for the receipts. He never asked for anything.

But we couldn't go over to the feast table, not yet, Momo said, because that would kill the mood. We had to go inside and change first, and we weren't allowed to be in the same room because that would ruin it too. No one else was allowed to see when each of us put on our costume and we had to spend some time alone with our reflection first, Momo said.

Bella and I nodded eagerly. We were each given a paper bag, Momo took hers and we spread out in Bella's house. We took care not to be near the dad in the living room and we made sure to close the doors behind us because it felt important somehow, what Momo had said: We had to leave our selves behind in the rooms, so that none of our usual selves could slip out.

I looked into the paper bag. While Momo was measuring our bodies we decided that no one could represent anyone who already existed. Then everything would be predetermined: the dialogue would already be there, the gestures, facial expressions, the attitudes, it wouldn't be what we wanted it to be. So Momo sewed three costumes, Bella and I helped at first but we hadn't been allowed to see the results. However we begged and pleaded Momo had just shaken her head and said that we had to wait until it was time.

I wriggled, shimmied, and twisted to get into that strange garment. Then I looked in the mirror.

The fabric was silvery and thick, the lower part was a cross between pants and a skirt and reached all the way down to the floor, like samurai pants. The upper part was an armor. Small, stiff, octagonal pieces made up the chest plate, smoothing my peaked girl-breasts into a flat chest. I thought about the *Brothers Lionheart*, and of Tengil who had frightened me so when I was small. I stroked the stiff glimmering material cautiously, imagining that I was a conqueror of a world somewhere across the universe. For a second I thought it was childish to dream of such things when you were about to turn fourteen and the image of Momo's mother appeared in my mind, how she had peeked in while we were planning and cutting and tacking. She came into our world with her large nimble hands and her eagle eye and when she touched the materials it was like I had a grown-up-eye too because then I could see the fabric scraps were crooked, the armor was just silver-painted cardboard and the pieces were held together with rubber bands. I hated her then. I wanted to bare my teeth and growl at her, tell her she wasn't allowed to be here, that she was ruining everything.

I pushed away the memory of Momo's mother, my stomach still felt fine and suddenly I had the urge to sing. Surely my voice would sound different if I opened my mouth, it would be strong and dark and beautiful. But I kept my mouth shut, I didn't want to let anything out because I wasn't finished yet. In the paper bag was the mask Momo had cast. I took it out, turned it around my hands remembering the feeling of the cold, wet plaster and how itchy it was when it dried, how my skin took a deep breath when Momo gently pried it off my face. I pulled the thin rubber band and fitted the mask over my face. It stretched across my scalp, burning, but when I looked out of my new eye sockets, when I caught sight of my whole new self in the mirror, the pain didn't matter.

I had the face of a bird. I couldn't really put my finger on how she had pulled it off, there was something to the way she'd built up my nose and cheekbones, something in the way the peppercorn eyes were painted on. My new skin glittered as I turned my head, and I thought about silvery gray feather costumes, of cranes raising their beaks to the sky and their long, serpentine necks, and then I knew that the creature in the mirror was me, and Kim was no more.

I cracked open the door, snuck out, and looked for the others. At first I couldn't see them any-where, but once in the garden I caught sight of a shadow over by the greenhouse. It was almost dark by then, the candles flickered, the shadows were still. I followed the stone path, feeling the wide pants legs brush my calves as I moved.

Out of the corner of my eye I saw the veranda door slowly glide open and someone came strid-ing across the grass. We went over to the green-house and the sunken table, we crossed the stones and grass and the whole time there was a kind of music in the air, a delicate, shimmering sound singing us onward, emptying us of our old selves with each step we took.

We were so beautiful.

We were so beautiful!

Among the flickering candles, the Desert Creature stood. At first, I didn't know his name, I'd never seen anyone of his kind before, but as he stood there in front of me his name became clear. He wore a sand-colored, slim-fitting tuxedo, the arms were three-quarter length and he had thick metal bracelets on his wrists. His nails were painted black and filed to sharp points, his thick hair was pulled through a wide steel cylinder at the top of his head and it cascaded like a waterfall. His plaster mask was fastened with a thick, dark-brown leather band around his head. The face had whiskers but the eyes and mouth were human, neatly painted in shiny lacquer colors. He bowed down when we came near, I bowed back and when I turned my head I saw that it was Pierrot walking over the grass. I mean, it *wasn't* Pierrot, we'd already decided that, but he was the first one who came to mind because the creature coming toward us was wearing a checkered costume with lace at the throat. He had a peaked hat with round buttons and a lacquered mask that looked like porcelain, large circles of rouge on his cheeks, sorrowful doll eyes, and a little mustache.

Pierrot and the Desert Creature bowed to each other. Pierrot and I bowed to each other. Then we went to table, ceremoniously with our heads held high. We had extraordinary fun that first night. We ate and ate the cookies and fruit, we drank the sweet tea and because the night stretched on we were buzzing with sugar and darkness. From all of Bella's flowers rose the night scent and we danced together under the stars. We made up songs and held each other's hands, dancing chain dances around the greenhouse, which was reflecting the moonshine so strangely and the Desert Creature cupped his paws around his mouth and howled at the sky like a coyote. When we couldn't dance anymore we collapsed into a heap on the grass. We were enfolded in the smell of sweat and makeup and plaster and if I could've, if I had been able to freeze a moment in my life and hang it up on the wall, then it would've been this one with Pierrot, the Desert Creature, and the Avian Conqueror, lying there with our bellies full of goodies, happily exhausted by the endless possibilities of the game.

IT WAS LIKE Bella was obsessed with that strange flower. She examined every centimeter, she had a little loupe and a kit full of mini tweezers and scalpels with which to prod and pinch. I stood beside her in the humid greenhouse listening to her mutter. She gently opened up the petals, scraped off clumps of yellow pollen from the interior. Then she held the tip of the scalpel to the light, squinting around the loupe.

"Indeed!"

She pushed the petals aside, leaving enough space for me.

"She only has carpels, no stamen. See?"

I shook my head. The flower's insides were a golden mess of peaks and towers and I couldn't make sense of it. Bella pointed with the scalpel.

"These small buds, they mean she's female."

I was surprised.

"Haven't we known that all along?"

She smiled.

"Not really. We just thought so."

She put the loupe to her eye again, and said to herself:

"I didn't think so. No, I did not."

I watched Bella drive the scalpel into her head, carving loose a carpel and placing it on a small glass tray. The flower swayed, and my stomach tingled.

"She doesn't like it, Bella. She wants you to stop."

Bella gave me a stern look, her voice was gentle but firm.

"She's fine."

Then she smiled and handed me the scalpel.

"Want to try?"

Warily I took the sharp tool, weighed it in my hand. Bella smiled encouragingly.

"It's not hard."

She parted the corolla, making room for me in front of the large head. I looked down into the insides and tried to sharpen my gaze. It was like dunking your head underwater, unnaturally sharp contours that made my eyes burn. Bella's voice seemed to be coming from far far away.

"Do you see those tiny sacs?"

I looked. At the base of the carpels were small, teensy orbs, no larger than a clove. They looked tense and swollen, the thin membrane strained. I nodded softly.

"Cut one open so we can find out what's inside."

I put the tip to one of the thin membranes, pressed gently and the sharp metal slid right into the sac. It popped like a balloon and out flowed a thick amber liquid. A sweet smell rose up to my nostrils. Bella snatched the scalpel from me and leaned in to get a proper look.

"Fantastic!"

She inspected the sharp tip, dipped her nail in the liquid, put it to her nose and sniffed.

"Like honey!"

She started doggedly flipping through one of her thick books, opened it up and showed me a color spread. There was was a full-page picture of a butterfly with whitish pale, brown-blasted wings, and a nasty fuzzy caterpillar body. Magnified, its head was grotesque: unseeing compound eyes, its long trunk rolled up at the bottom, like a peculiar musical instrument. Bella pointed at the trunk, leaving a spot of yellow nectar on the page.

"That's as sharp as a nail. The butterfly pokes holes in the sacs and draws the liquid out, like a syringe. But it takes a long time, sometimes it has to suck at it for minutes at a time. That's when the pollen fastens here, see?"

She pointed. I nodded. Its legs were barbed, like a crab's.

"And then?"

Bella shut the book, sighing.

"Then you hope there's a male flower nearby that the butterfly can land on next. Who knows how we're going to find one of those."

THE AIR WAS warm, the gravel sun-baked, and gym was the last class of the day. Of course we played baseball—boys' choice—and Bella, Momo, and I were like stragglers out on the field. Taking hardly a step in any direction, barely reaching up an arm, never laying a hand on the ball.

It wasn't that we didn't like the game. We played it at home sometimes, on the blind alley behind Momo's house. Then we cracked the bat with all our might and scored a run almost every time. But here it was different. Here the boys followed even our slightest movements. They saw everything, ready to pounce on any opportunity with a grin and comment. Momo had long, strong legs but she didn't use them. She shuffled around, trying to make herself as gray and invisible as possible. I stood there, arms crossed, and didn't even blink when the teacher shouted at me to come on and make some sort of effort, for the team's sake.

Bella's breasts swung when she moved, no T-shirt in the world was big enough to conceal them, and when she ran, when she gained speed and really tried to do her best, for the team's sake, the next thing you'd hear was wolf whistles and applause from the boys.

Bella stopped running, her throat and cheeks aflame. A voice from the chorus screamed:

"Over here, baby, let me cop a feel!"

My stomach turned. For a second I thought about the giant from my daydreams, imagining myself striding across the field and picking up the boys with my giant-hands, and throwing them in a wide arc across the town. But my body was a lanky girl-body and I looked at the ground, swallowing in an attempt to keep the nausea from making its way up my throat.

The teacher stood there with his whistle. He heard and saw everything but didn't flinch. He put the whistle to his mouth and blew, the hour was up, the players dispersed. The teacher gestured to Momo and me to collect the bats and cones and carry them off to the equipment room. This was a sort of punishment. If you didn't try hard enough during gym class, you had to clean up. Everyone was aware of who he'd chosen, which was the point, you were supposed to feel exposed. Momo sucked it up and did what he wanted, but I hung back and looked for Bella. She was walking to the changing room, head hanging low. I caught up with her, grabbed her by the shoulders. Then she stopped and gave me a feeble smile.

"They're babies!"

I wanted to smile back, I wanted to give a comforting nod, say "I know, what dorks, forget about them." But I couldn't smile. This wasn't child's play, not even close. The boys were already too used to getting to have their way with us with no consequences. The lump of nausea loosened in my throat, came out as a stream of speech:

"We should—someone should rip on them. Beat it out of them. So they never do it again."

Bella looked at me, her eyes flashed with surprise. Then she shrugged.

"Oh. I just want to take a shower. And go home."

She linked arms with me. We walked toward the schoolhouse and when we came around the corner, they were standing outside the door, waiting.

I stopped, but Bella didn't. It was like she'd suddenly decided to object, they didn't have the right to scare her anymore. She lifted her chin, didn't cross her arms, let them hang loose at her sides. She walked straight up to the boys and for a moment I thought they were going to scatter, they were going to let her through.

I didn't hear what they said, I just heard the tone, their soft fake voices. And they let her into the group, they let her take several steps toward the door before they started touching her, pushing their bodies close, slipping their hands under her shirt for a feel, Bella trying to twist out of their grip, but the boys wouldn't let go of her clothes. They yanked and shoved until they were holding up her T-shirt and sports bra like trophies, waving the fabric in the air, laughing, pointing.

Bella was only a few meters away.

She was covering her bare breasts, her hair was in her face, her shoulders hunched. She pressed her breasts to her body and stood perfectly still.

It happened so fast. I didn't manage to do anything while it was happening, but now my legs unfroze and I rushed ahead. I screamed that they were cocksuckers and bastards and had no right to do this, you fucks, *You have no right to do this!*

For the boys, the game was over. They weren't looking at Bella anymore and they didn't care about me at all. They dumped her clothes in my arms then turned their backs to us, walked off to their changing room like nothing had happened.

I handed Bella her clothes. She fumbled them, dropped her bra on the asphalt and let it be there, then pulled her shirt over her head. She stood there hugging herself. I stroked her hair, her cheeks.

Bella, my lovely Bella, don't let them get under your skin, don't let them get to you!

Bella was fighting back tears, clenching her teeth, pressing her hands to her eyes. Her nostrils quivered, a string of snot slid over her upper lip. I held her and rubbed her back. Out of the corner of my eye I saw Momo come out of the equipment room. As soon as she laid eyes on us she started running, she saw Bella's bra on the asphalt and didn't ask any questions, all she did was put her arms around us.

We stood there hugging, comforting each other with our bodies. Our hearts beat close together and I don't know if it was my heart or Bella's, if it was my pulse or hers that was pounding so hard, but it was minutes before our breath returned to its usual rhythm.

AFTER THAT DAY, it was a week before we so much as caught a glimpse of Momo. She wasn't at school and in the afternoons she worked on her sewing behind closed blinds. I walked past her house. There were a few times I considered knocking, but didn't. We felt the same way: this was urgent. The boys' faces, Bella hugging herself. The image came to me each night when I shut my eyes, and I longed for another chance to put a mask between myself and the world, to wear a costume that turned me into someone else, and stop being the Kim who'd just stood there on the schoolyard.

The school days passed. Bella and I walked through the corridors, eyes glazed, and shrugged when teachers asked us where Momo was. Late one Friday night, I was in bed. Moonlight was spilling through the window like a flashlight's beam, and I was writhing in the sheets because my skin was sensitive and the linens were rough. Suddenly a little piece of paper sailed in through the crack of my window. A short, pithy message:

Finished now. Tomorrow night! /M.

I put the note under my pillow. That night I dreamt of butterflies.

IT WAS A balmy night, spring had begun its slide into summer, the trees' leaves were thick and bright green. We didn't speak—we met each other's eyes and accepted the paper bags that Momo ceremoniously handed to us. When I opened my bag in Bella's room, my heart started hammering in my ears.

She'd made me a tiger costume. There was a hooded coat and a pair of elbow-length gloves, each finger tipped with a golden claw. There was no mask, no plaster to hide my face, but she'd painted dark-brown filigree lines on a thin nylon stocking. I pulled the stocking over my face and put the hood on. I looked in the mirror.

A shriek escaped me and hit the glass, it bounced sharply between the walls. Only when it died away could I take a proper look. Shere Khan shimmered in the mirror. He glared at me with glowing yellow eyes, his face dark and threatening. The wide coat and hood obscured my usual gestures and when I moved, he moved too, but not like a girl with a pimply back and a body full of worry. He moved like a king, and we were one and the same, he and me.

Yes, Momo had really outdone herself. As I walked toward the garden feeling the heft of the coat, I realized that she had planned every last detail of this evening. Lanterns illuminated the greenhouse and apparently she'd managed to get hold of a large stereo because pounding drums and dark rhythms spilled from the greenhouse, an undulating melody that made me think of gold and the glinting whites of eyes. She greeted us inside the greenhouse, the site of the party, and as I came closer I saw an Explorer standing by the wooden table, sporting a white safari hat and a waxed mustache. I glimpsed the mysterious flower's head through the doorway; it was nodding gently as if craning her neck to get a good look at us. The terrace door opened and the Explorer laughed with delight as a Silverback entered. He walked with the help of his knuckles, and when he was very close he unleashed a howl, and I couldn't help but join in on the laughter.

The Explorer bowed, and with a sweep of his gloved hand he gestured to the table.

"Welcome to the tropics, my friends. Dinner is served."

It was a clear, starry night. We lay on the lawn outside the greenhouse, resting our heads on each other's stomachs. Momo had taken off her safari hat, her hair rippled over my tiger-chest. The flowers around us had opened up, their soft interiors gleaming in the darkness. She looked at us through the doorway, her face was open and smooth and it made me think of butterflies, how their pointy proboscises pierced sacs of nectar, how they sucked it in. I propped myself up on my elbow and raised my cup of tea with a practiced gesture.

"Would it please the gentlemen to add a few true drops to the brew?"

I moved Momo's head off my stomach. She looked up with surprise when I wrapped my coat around me, walked up to the flower and started inspecting the teeming vessels in the center of its head. They seemed to be tiny blisters enclosed in the petals, straining and aching and filled with something that needed to get out.

Bella stood up in her unwieldy gorilla costume. Her spirits had been high all night. She'd either been howling like a gorilla or howling with laughter, and now she was so hoarse and tired that she was swaying over to the greenhouse.

"Oh, yes! New life will course through our bodies, and the stars will take our secrets to the grave!"

Momo giggled. She couldn't help it. Bella was striding comically across the flagstones. The pants of the gorilla costume had hitched themselves up, revealing her tube socks. But Bella shot her a stern look and Momo got hold of herself and said:

"We shall make a pact, gentlemen. We shall brew a Magical Potion and drink together. We shall never speak of our drink to any mortal, whatever may come!"

And as she spoke, she raised her cup of tea to the heavens, and we raised ours as well. Bella skipped toward me and guided the flower's head downward.

"Yes, I swear, I swear!"

We swore our oaths and I pierced one of the blisters with my index finger's claw.

Thick nectar seeped out.

One drop for each glass.

We toasted. Then we gulped down the tea, suddenly irresistibly sweet and spicy. And when we looked up from our cups, when we looked at each other, a deep silence engulfed us.

WITHOUT A WORD, we walked through the garden, into Bella's bedroom. We stood in front of her mirrored wardrobe doors and undressed. We peeled our garments off in slow motion. We let them fall, gazing tenderly at our reflection, tenderly down at our bodies. We could barely breathe, looking at what was in the mirror, our eyes did all the talking, it was like they were asking: "Is it true, what we're seeing, is this really happening, or will we wake up and vomit and remember everything as if it had been a dream?"

The three of us stood there naked, in a bedroom with smoky mirrored doors inside a townhouse. Our breasts were gone and the roundness of our hips had straightened out, the tendons and muscles of our shoulders and arms were different, visible under our skin. Our throats and necks were wider, and in the middle of our throats were

Adam's apples as large as ripe plums. I swallowed and it sat in my throat, a heavy, bobbing float. Our stomachs had hollowed out, the fat under our skin was gone, and there was no slit between our legs anymore. The hair was still there, sparse and so delicate it hurt when stroked against the grain, and beneath that little bush, between our thighs, we each had a penis. Soft skin covered the glans and under it hung a wrinkled sack of skin with two oval stones inside.

Momo was the first to open her mouth, her voice was rougher than usual and cracked with a screech at the last syllable.

"My God."

She grabbed it and it filled with a rush of blood. I watched her balls contract and she opened her eyes wide.

"It's like, like . . ."

I wrapped my hand around my own and felt a faint tickle in my stomach.

"Like a baby bird."

When I spoke, my voice scratched my throat, like I'd swallowed a strand of hair. Our new lives were in our hands. We looked at our new bodies, we flexed and stretched our new limbs and we felt something fresh in our blood. We gazed at our boy-bodies, reached out our hands, touched the surface of the mirror and our eyes lit up, flashing like lightning in the glass.

I RAN DOWN the street through the night. My legs were pure power and speed and strength. The soles of my feet hit the asphalt and each step felt like the bounce of a trampoline, a leap into the air, the breathtaking feeling of flight. Like being born again, like my body had shed all past memories, and had emerged onto an invisible, unknown path.

I ran, and Bella and Momo ran behind me, laughing and shouting, and I recognized their voices, even though they didn't sound like themselves. Momo caught up with me. Her boy-face barely resembled her, but I knew who it was. Maybe it was in the eyes or the facial expressions, or how her smile split her face as she outran me. She was prancing and reaching her arms into the air, as if the whole world was suddenly there to do her bidding.

We arrived in the center of town, the neon lights glittering. We walked three-by-three. We didn't talk—we didn't need to talk. The wonder was pounding inside me, I listened as Momo drank in the air and smells, I watched Bella flex her muscles.

We encountered boys. Made eye contact for a fraction of a second, then they sort of just looked past us, past our eyes. It was strange. No slick, slippery looks, no desire, no grins, nothing that crept under our skin and sank its teeth in. Just a glazed, distant look that neither looked at nor looked away.

We encountered girls but didn't know what to do with their glances. Instinctively we looked at the ground, and I thought that this reality we were walking around in was madness, what had happened to us was impossible, it absolutely couldn't have happened, and yet it had. It wasn't a dream, it wasn't a game. Strangers looked at us and their gazes were different. Our new bodies were reflected in them. It was unbelievable, this dizzying thought took hold and left me reeling.

I had to steady myself on Momo's shoulder, and Momo put his arm around me. An arm around my waist, my arm around his neck and our bodies, that feeling, Momo's body hard and boy-soft against mine—another hole in reality opened up, so like an abyss that I immediately let go of him and laughed it off. A nervous laugh that charged the air with a rollicking energy. I ran a few steps, careening like a foal, grabbed hold of Momo's jacket and chased him down the street until I forgot the feeling, the one that was so unreal it was impossible to parse.

DAWN BROKE ON the horizon, a stretch of forest separated the city from the plains and we kneeled among the spruce trees. Among the bilberry bushes, we sat. The damp worked its way into our jeans and we held each other's hands. Our noses ran because the cold morning was raw and damp. Momo's forearms had been scratched by the slender, dry tree branches and my knee was swollen, my pant leg was rolled up and the skin was bluish red and a little bloody. I licked my upper lip to prevent the snot from running, felt the short spiky fluff growing there.

We sat in a tight circle, gripping each other's boy-hands. We'd spent the night intoxicated by enchantment, but now the light was on its way.

We were exhausted, but we didn't dare shut our eyes, we didn't dare lose sight of each other.

We had a feeling, a bad feeling: falling asleep would have dire consequences.

I shivered with cold and exhaustion. Momo held my hand, clasped it. His voice crackled, it was a boy's voice, and even though I'd been hearing it all night, it startled me.

"Do you think we're going to die?"

We were silent. I thought of my parents, about how they'd have to file a missing person's report at the police station, but that I'd never be found, I'd be a cold case. Momo's parents and Bella's dad, everyone would wonder. Sooner or later someone would find the three unidentifiable boys in the forest. They might be able to trace our clothing, but then . . . It was impossible to think beyond that, it jumbled in my mind because it was so unthinkable, what had happened.

What was happening.

But I didn't say any of the things I was thinking, I tried to steady my voice:

"Of course we won't."

Bella's eyes were bloodshot. His boy-lip quivered, out of exhaustion, cold, and fear.

"Maybe we're hallucinating. Maybe we're just passed out on the lawn back home. Maybe everything is the same as always."

I didn't answer. I just focused on the large lump bobbing in my throat even though my mouth was bone-dry. Momo crept even closer to me and put his arm around my waist. I pressed myself against his warm body, the tears burned and begged to fall. Bella came closer, too. Our boy-faces were close together, I saw their pores and hairs and moles but I tried to focus on their eyes, nothing more.

Tears fell from Bella's greenish-gray, fright-tired eyes.

Momo held me tightly:

"If we die. If we die now, then at least we'll die together."

And Bella managed a weak smile through his tears and nodded. I felt their pulses pounding in their lithe, sinewy bodies, and thought, "Yes, if I'm going to die, I might as well die now, here, with you." Momo's breath caressed my face and Bella's cheek pressed against my neck, Momo's sharp shoulder jutted into mine and we whispered in unison, "If this is death, if what we've done is take our own lives, then that's what's going to happen, now, sitting here, close together." And once we'd said that, it was like something released inside of us. Our bodies softened and I took a long breath—our lungs filled to their breaking point and expanded our slender boy-ribs.

The last thing I remember is lying with my cheek against Bella's sweet, acrid armpit.

When I woke, rays of sunshine probed the spaces between the jagged spruce branches. I opened my eyes, my body was cold and tender and damp. The bright sky high above came through in blue patches. I raised my head, groaning, propped myself up on my elbow and looked around. And then I remembered. I remembered every minute of the day before, the game and the intoxication and the fear, and I bit my tongue when I looked at the others. I bit it so hard I tasted blood. When I opened my mouth and shrieked, my voice was as clear and shrill as I remembered it.

I was awake. This was my usual reality. We

weren't dead. We were wet and dirty, but we weren't dead. It wasn't death that had come for us, it was something else, something incomprehensible, but now everything was back to normal. The boy-bodies had softened away, our shapes were girl-shapes and my shouts rang through the trees. I cried out and hollered and hysterically waved my arms in the air. Bella and Momo woke, sleep still in their eyes. I saw their memories return, their faces light up when they realized they were alive.

We hugged each other tightly, Bella, Momo, and I. We hugged each other and laughed and cried a little, too, we jumped up and down with joy and excitement. Bella ran her hands over her breasts, looked down at them fondly. Her gaze and touch were loving.

When the excitement waned, when the ache in our bodies had reasserted itself, we sat back down on the ground. We kept our heads close together, spoke to each other earnestly, in low voices. Momo looked at us with wide eyes and said, "We have to promise, on our honor, that we will never tell a living soul about this. We have to promise!"

And so we promised. We nodded, swearing that this was our secret, and Momo laughed in spite of all the seriousness, because we were as dirty as trolls and because the whole thing was so nuts, nuts and unbelievable and fantastic. I laughed, too, and Bella looked up between the spruce branches, she squinted at the morning sun and then fished her watch out of her jeans pocket.

"It's only six. No one will notice a thing."

And she was right. Inside the townhouse, Bella's dad was asleep in front of the TV. The flickering screen cast a blue glow through the doorway and we padded past him and snuck into the bathroom. We tore off our disheveled, dirty clothes. I touched my knee. It was sore, but it was no longer bruised and neither Momo nor I still had scratches on our forearms. We scrubbed our hands and faces, combed the needles and chaff from our hair.

In the mirror, three familiar girl-faces looked back at us, but they had new eyes.

I WAKE UP early. The wind is high, the garden is swishing, and the wooden walls are creaking. The dream lingers in my mind and I try to bat it away, I don't want to remember, not yet. "Do you hear me!" I shout into the room. "I don't want to!" But there is no one here but me and the forest and house, and the images are trying to get in:

I'm walking through the woods, branches scratch my face. I tuck my head to dodge dry twigs and when I look back up, the forest isn't there anymore. I'm standing on asphalt, a glass house in front of me, it's burning, the window panes clatter as they break. With my arm I shield myself from the shards and heat. Someone in there is on fire, I see a face: eyes shut, mouth wide-open. I rush in. It might be me screaming or it's her voice I hear, and before I wake up I look straight into her interior, burnt white.

I'm making porridge. It smells good, the wood burning in the stove crackles and snaps. Outside, the sun is rising between the trunks and the twigs with which the wind is having its way. My stomach craves carbohydrates. I burn my tongue and throat because I can't wait. The energy courses through my body like glowing threads, my legs are restless and I run out to my strongest tree. I jump up, grab hold of a thick branch, hang like an orangutan, arms stretched, feet inches above the ground. The branches sway with my weight, it's pleasing, I heave myself up, my chin grazes the rough bark but I'm in perfect control, my muscles are pushing their limits. I do ten chin-ups, fifteen, twenty, the lactic acid pulses through my arms. I do ten more and shut my eyes. All I feel is pain. Then the adrenaline kicks in, a red explosion behind my eyes. I do another ten and hear myself holler each time my chin reaches over the branch. I let go and let my body fall.

It's so good, it's so good.

The fatigue, the relief, the taste of blood.

Eyes shut, I lie on a brown carpet of last-year's leaves, resting deep inside myself. My breathing evens out and the images in my head become clear.

Bella and Momo, their fourteen-year-old faces.

It's been an eternity since I've seen them. I haven't counted the days, haven't cared that the months keep unfolding. How their lives have been, I don't know, but years don't go by unnoticed. I imagine Bella as a round-cheeked young woman, freckled and curvy. I smile to myself, her eyes are still clear and intelligent. And Momo is a beauty, dark and strong.

Or maybe it's not like that, is this just wishful thinking?

Maybe life has ground them down. Maybe their tired faces are grooved with lines even though they're still young.

Like me.

No, I can't imagine them. They've grown up,

outgrown me, grown apart from me. But we still have our shared history.

I open my eyes. The shushing wind carries an echo of Bella's voice, of what she said on the phone:

You owe us that.

I pack the last of the cans into a tote bag. The car smells of damp and old sweat. The old engine sputters to life after months of being parked, hacking for a few seconds before it finds its rhythm. I check the rearview mirror; the roof and the rain gutters, the doors, the stairs to the entry-way. Along the wall, the snowdrops have begun to bloom. I put the car in one, the tires reluctantly gain traction on the gravel. The morning sun flashes on the hood as I come around the bend and my pulse speeds in pace with the accelerator, its beating and thumping makes my fingers prickle.

I drive north.

THREE BOYS WALKED through town. It was the very first week of summer vacation. Down the avenues we walked, then across the cobbled square. We walked down the tree-lined passages, dark with night, along the gravel paths running between the park lawns. It was swarming with boys. They stood between the trees, they sat cross-legged in circles and between them the glow of cigarettes flashed like fireflies in the dark. They held beer cans in their sinewy hands and spoke in low voices. Now and then they unleashed a flock of raspy laughter that soared up into the trees, black sharp-eyed birds perching among the leaves.

We walked, hands shoved deep into our pockets. We didn't say much because we were still unsure of our new voices and were sneaking glances at the groups of boys on the lawns. Then we strayed from the gravel path and sat down a little out of the way. We had neither cigarettes nor beer with which to busy our hands, so we tore up fistfuls of grass, tearing them into itsy-bitsy pieces that fell like confetti between our feet and the dew crept through our denim. With her boy-voice Momo said that it was suh-weet that school was out and it was so obviously a boy-line that the three of us, we burst out laughing and the wind lifted the wings of our laughter, which mixed with the other boy-laughs that had flown up into the trees. And my laughter flew highest of all, all the way over to the next group of boys it went and there someone looked up, a dark shield of a cap's brim that rose above the rest, a pair of eyes that glimmered. He tore himself away and became his own boy-figure strolling across the grass, over to us. The group he'd been sitting with fell silent, the voices became whispers and my heart hardened in my chest, pounded against my ribs. He wore tough military boots and when he crouched down next to me I saw that his leather jacket was worn and scratched. He pushed his cap up to his forehead; in his hand was an unlit cigarette.

"Do you smoke?"

I shook my head, didn't dare let my boy-voice out. He gave my arm a shove and raised his voice enough for me to hear its edge.

"Sure, you fuckin' smoke!"

"No, I don't."

My boy-voice left me before I was ready, and I shut my mouth in horror. In the air in front of me, I could see the blunt contours of the words and it was so strange. He fished another cigarette out of his breast pocket and handed it to me.

"Tonight you do."

I looked at the cigarette, white against the darkness. I took it from him and put it between my lips; he grinned, fished out a lighter from his pants pocket, lit both cigarettes, and took a deep drag. I took a drag, too. The smoke tore at my lungs and I did what Momo and I had done behind her parents' garage, exhaling gently so as not to start coughing. And none of us said anything because we didn't know what to say, that must have been why, because our silence was a secure and familiar signal, he reached his hand out to me and said:

"Tony."

And I said my name using my boy-voice and it became a boy-name. The vowels became a tightly stretched string and I liked it, it sounded better coming from a boy-mouth than out of my usual one. Tony squeezed my hand and nodded encouragingly toward the other two. Momo understood and said her name and it also became a boy's, dark and rattling. Bella said nothing, her eyes fixed on the grass. Tony raised his eyebrows, underneath them his eyes hardened. I snatched blindly at something in the air. A neon yellow name was winding itself high up the building facades and I reached for it, took it down from the sky for Bella.

"That's Mack."

I shoved her arm, forcing her to look up at Tony. Her eyes were weak with fear. She wanted to avoid his gaze, she was expecting it to glide over her round breasts and for the words to stream from his mouth, sharp, poisonous words that stuck to her pale skin.

But Tony's gaze didn't glide, because there was

nothing to glide across. He reached out his hand, wrapped his rough fingers around her earth-covered ones and I watched his shoulder muscles move underneath his jacket as they greeted each other. He didn't say anything to her, he turned to me.

"You live around here?"

I tossed my head.

"Out west."

He nodded to the group sitting behind him.

"We live across the bridge."

I looked toward the harbor. The bridge's lights were like pearls strung across the water.

"Nice."

Tony gave me a searching look. I went cold inside, words weren't easy. My thoughts took shape in my boy-mouth and I didn't know how they would sound, what he would think, what would happen if I crossed one of the many lines surrounding my new body like blue lasers. But Tony's face broke open into what was almost a smile.

"You're each gonna get a beer."

We sat with the boys. The beer loosened our vocal cords and the black laughter birds flocked for no reason at all. Our boy-hands gripped theirs, strong fingers and quick jerk of their forearm, sometimes so hard I thought my elbow would get disjointed. To avoid the pain you had to jerk back, gripping his hand just as hard as he was gripping mine. Then the energy of the movement locked between us, an electric tension in our hands as they said their names.

And Tony.

His rough hand holding the beer can, a heavy silver ring on his thumb, a faded green tattoo across the back of his hand with twisting details that wound underneath his jacket sleeve. His steely blue eyes flashed under the bill of his cap, and I wanted to bow my head in front of him, wanted his eyes to wash over me like cold water.

THAT NIGHT I stood in front of the mirror in my bedroom for a long time. It was just before dawn and the exhaustion was lurking behind my eyelids, but I fought it. I didn't want to go back, not yet.

I stood naked, feet together, arms at my sides. In the mirror was a boy, and he was looking back at me.

My own face had always been beneath Momo's masks. My girl-eyes were what was looking through the holes in the plaster. It was my girl-body, deep underneath the fabric and seams, that made the mirror image move. But the boy in the mirror didn't have a costume to take off. The skin was my skin and yet another's. I ran my fingers over my arms and the back of my hands, examining my knuckles, the strong tendons. There was no excess skin, no clothing layers bunching into sausages, revealing you as someone to be stepped on, stepped over. My new skin fit like skin should fit. It stretched perfectly across my boy-hands as I clenched and opened them, turning them around and taking them in, using them to stroke my soft stomach. I touched my belly button, my finger nudged the warm skin, the roughness of my fingertip. My pelvic bone, inner thighs, the dark hair and what was in between: something that moved of its own accord at the very thought of touch.

I ran my hands down my inner thighs, grabbed hold of the balls. The penis filled with blood, grew in my hand, rubbed itself against my fingers. I'd often imagined this, before the first transformation. I didn't mean to, I couldn't help it, the thoughts just turned up at night. Images of boys, their naked bodies, hot skin, wet tongues. How it must feel to hold a penis and look a boy in the eyes. How my groin would feel when I saw what was there.

I looked my reflection in the eye and wanted him to touch me, I wanted him to reach his hands through the mirror and touch me. And I gripped it harder, pumping rhythmically up and down, feeling my hand around it and feeling it in my hand. It was a point of heat, a molten core, a center that gave me tunnel vision. Twitching, aching swells running upward and out, I drew a deep breath, biting my fingers so I wouldn't scream out loud.

I TOOK MY monthly allowance plus five hundred from my savings and went to the military surplus store. One pair of fourteen-hole boots cost 1100 kronor. I dragged my feet through the gravel all the way home just so he'd think I'd had them a long time.

DAWN.

We lay in the greenhouse. We were very tired but didn't want to go to sleep, not yet. That night's experiences were still pumping endorphins into our boy-bodies and the flower hadn't closed up. She lapped greedily at the darkness and she shone so fantastically, like a piece of violet fabric woven with glittering threads, the kind of fabric that actresses wear to the Oscars, fabric that glitters like a starry sky under the searchlights. But our flower didn't need a searchlight, no artificial suns. She glittered with her own power.

We could hardly keep our eyes open. Every now and then one of us giggled, the giggle was infectious and we all started giggling, laughing out loud and in unison before it died down as suddenly as it had begun. Momo's head was in my lap, one hand in the water trough. Her body was limp and still with fatigue and adventure, but Bella propped herself up on her elbow and rested her chin in her palm. She was transfixed by the flower and sounded serious when she spoke.

"We should tell someone. About what she can do."

I thought about E.T., of men in white air-tight uniforms and crackling walkie-talkie voices and in the dusk I heard my own voice, suddenly very clear and wakeful.

"No, we can't! Of course we can't, you know what would happen."

Momo gave a little sigh, her chest heaved in my lap. My diaphragm tingled because it felt so strange, everything was so sensitive. So new.

Bella was overcome with sadness.

"I know. But still. Imagine if people found out. It would be different. *Everything* would be different."

It was silent and in the silence the three of us must have drifted off to sleep because when I opened my eyes the next day it was light and Momo's dark hair was flowing across my lap, her shirt stretched across her breasts and I didn't feel anything in my diaphragm, nothing moving between my legs.

BELLA'S BOY-BODY SAT next to mine at
the back of the bus.

Had our classmates taken the time to get to
know the girl with the old soul who so seldom
spoke during class, had they had taken the slightest interest in her life, they would've seen what a
resource she was. She was fourteen years old, tran-
quil and proper, her dad's credit card stowed in
the inside pocket of her schoolbag. When something ran out at home she took her bike and her
bag and went to the mini-mart. The shop assis-
tants knew why this little red-haired teenager was
at the shelves in their shop several times a week,
comparing the 'prices for coffee, cereal, and deter-
gent. Everyone smiled at her, helped her pack her
bags, carried them out to her bicycle basket.

Of course there were age limits. The other
teenagers in the area were strictly forbidden to

buy cigarettes and beer. But Bella had privileges. She was chubby, her front teeth were too big and her dad didn't care about her. He was a wretch who couldn't get a handle on his life and would probably die prematurely because of all the pills and junk he stuffed into himself. When Bella got to the cashier, when she heaved up a six-pack of beer onto the belt and pointed at the cigarettes, the cashiers regarded her with mildness and pity and let her buy whatever she asked for.

At first Bella didn't want to come along. Momo had to spend ages convincing her before she gave in and even then she was a little grumpy, pouting like a small child. "What are we supposed to do with them?" she said. "What fun is there in sitting and listening to their robber stories all night? They're full of shit, if you ask me." I didn't say anything because there was so much inside me that I couldn't explain. Tony's voice was ringing in my head. Before we parted he'd given us a time and location. "You'll be there tomorrow," he'd said. "We're going on an adventure." All morning, all day and all night I'd walked around in a daze, full of dread and anticipation. Tony's voice followed every step I took, like a point of light, a flashlight beam at night.

But for Momo, it was simple. She threw an arm around Bella's shoulders, laughing softly and infectiously. "Lighten up, it's just a game," she said. "A ramble, an excursion. We're the Three Musketeers, or have you forgotten that? We are spies on a mission inside enemy lines, we are shrewd infiltrators with the right to steal the foreign military's secret knowledge, we are . . ."

Bella smiled a crooked smile, raised her hand.

"Fine, I get it. Let's go."

So there we were, on the bus, with a bag full of beer and cigarettes. Bella sighed and cocked her curly, red-haired boy-head.

"I wonder what they're going to do."

I grinned.

"What *we* will do, Mack. What *we* will do!"

Bella glared at me.

"That stupid name. Couldn't you have come up with something better?"

I looked down at my steel-capped boots. She was right. It wasn't for me to name her. That was wrong, that would never have been allowed in any of our other games. But Tony's voice and Bella, she'd just been sitting there all quiet and pale! I wanted to put my hand on her arm, explain why I'd done what I'd done, but I caught sight of my own fingers. They were rough and sinewy and didn't seem fit to touch anyone. My hand stayed in my lap, my gaze found its way out the window.

"Don't hold the beers in your lap. They'll get all warm and gross."

TONY TOOK US with him.

To the vast industrial area on the other of the forest and the highway, to the last sliver of city before the city stopped. The disused shipyard at the mouth of the river with large rusty containers, empty or overflowing with relinquishments. There were long rows of forgotten warehouses, the necks of cranes stretched toward the bright night sky.

A few meters ahead we could see Tony's back. The soles of his boots soundless on the asphalt. The Hawk was right behind him. He too was large and heavy, but where Tony had muscles the Hawk had fat. His pale skin was like dishwater, his eyes were pig's eyes, his mouth was set in a twisted, ingratiating grin. Tony barely looked at him, barely talked to him. He just let him follow half a step behind, carrying that backpack filled with who knows what, but we would find out.

Tony strode through his land. Every now and then pointing at a building, a boat hull or a fence to indicate the space belonged to someone else, it was outside his territory and therefore forbidden ground. The glow of cigarettes flashed among the dark buildings. Out of the corner of my eye I caught shadows loosening themselves from the darkness high up in the old factory buildings, something shooting like an arrow from window to window, but when I turned my head I saw nothing.

We walked through the harbor landscape, past the rusting cranes and the abandoned docks. The night wind played with the decay, grabbing hold of metal that was about to crack, swinging it back and forth in a grating, moaning song. The forest lay ahead, a different kind of darkness flashed between the trees. Tony walked between the thick trunks. The Hawk held one hand in front of his face as protection, walking as though against a strong wind and we followed behind. The massive fir trees absorbed all the light given off by the night sky. I blindly moved my feet and branches whipped my face. There was light up ahead, for a moment Tony's back was a black silhouette against an open sky and then he was gone. We squeezed out of the forest and found ourselves on an outcrop a few meters above the inky river. To the west was the city, to the east a glimpse of the highway viaduct. Tony stood in a hollow in the mountain. His legs were hidden by brush and weeds and his hands were searching the stone wall, looking for something he knew was there. And then a gap opened up right into the rock, a door shaped like a cement block, lined with thick, dark metal. Tony climbed into the darkness. The Hawk stopped, gestured with his head so we would understand that we were supposed to go before him.

"Keep your mouths shut."

As usual this was not a threat, not a command. It was a fact, something we were finding out about ourselves in case we didn't already know. We looked at each other and Momo's hand grazed mine as we went in. Behind me I heard the Hawk shut the heavy door, the sound of a rusty bolt being shoved inside its hole.

After a few meters the room opened up. From the ceiling hung pale green sticks, a fluorescent, unnatural light. The mountain walls were scraggy. Junk was stacked in the corner, who knows what. Tony loomed in an armchair, an old-fashioned threadbare leather thing with stuffed arms. My head flooded with pictures of pirates, a robber's lair, treasure maps, and secret passageways, men who climbed up façades with knives clenched between their teeth. Yes, he sat like a robber baron in his chair, and the air had a stale smell that I couldn't yet identify. The sound from the forest in the water did not reach here, the hill absorbed them, never to let them go. Tony kept his gaze on his hands. The one hand squeezing the other, pressing the knuckles until they cracked. We didn't say anything. All we heard was the Hawk's grunting breath and the rustling of what he was taking out of the backpack.

That night we learned how to roast an oily piece of hash over a lighter, crumble it, mix it in cheap tobacco and roll the gauzy cigarette paper around the mixture. The Hawk put his tongue to the narrow strip of glue on the paper, showing how to run the tip of your tongue along the edge without getting cut. We learned how to puff it to life, keep it alive, close our lungs around the heavy smoke without choking. It was passed from hand to hand: the Hawk's fingers to Momo's, Momo's to Bella's, Bella's to Tony's, and from Tony's fingers (rough as sandpaper) to mine when I received the joint. I held it up at an angle as I had seen him do, pulled in the sharp smoke down my throat, down into my body. All the while he kept me in the corner of his eye, glancing without interest at Bella and Momo, but lingering on me.

The roach was so hot I burned my fingers, the smoke burned my tongue. Caution battled with the headrush: two snakes in an underwater dance, their long gleaming bodies entwined. It was like the drug never really took hold. The rush didn't turn into anything more than a dusky echo chamber deep inside myself, a sparkle in the corner of my eye, a bright aura that vanished as soon as I tried to catch sight of it. Momo and Bella gleamed weakly across from me and Tony's body had a violet glow against the leather chair. The Hawk's body was mute and lightless. He lay with his chin against the stone floor, eyes half shut, mouth drooling. All my fears burned away. The flame gasped and died, leaving only a ribbon of ashy smoke in the greenish light. We sat for a long time listening to the absence of sound. Then Tony got out of his chair. He didn't sway, didn't stumble, had no problem steadying his gaze. But in his eyes was new depth, new sight in those black pupils. Two bottomless wells that looked right at me, encouraging me to stand up and follow him out the door without looking back.

TONY LEANED AGAINST the building wall, holding his head down so that his face was hidden by the brim of his cap. An artery was pulsing on his neck but his breath was calm and controlled, voice deep and steady. In his hand was a pair of nippers.

"Keep an eye on the diode. If it starts blinking red then you better bolt."

I looked up at the window overhead. In the lower frame was a box with a light-emitting diode. It was flashing green. To one side of us was the wire mesh that surrounded the industrial area, on the other the forest towered. In the distance the fencing was split open, a long slit where someone had cut the fence open.

I looked at Tony, his chin, lips, hands. They were large man hands already, strong enough to pull apart a mesh of cut wire. For second I observed him, absorbing what I saw, letting my thoughts drift a bit too far from the now. I wasn't prepared. The hard push came from nowhere. I tumbled backward toward the wall and Tony was on top of me. Grabbing my lapels, his breath and the smell of smoke everywhere around me. That large body like a wall and my squished ribs. He dug his fists into my stomach, winding me. His voice growled in my ear:

"If the alarm goes off they'll be here in thirty seconds. I don't give a shit if you get caught."

I twisted away from his breath, glanced up at the diode box. The light wasn't green anymore, just an extinguished plastic globe and a vague crackle when the current no longer had anywhere to go. Tony kept his grip on my jacket. I should have been afraid. I should have torn myself away and run back to my own world, to the houses and gardens and my parents sleeping breaths.

But I stayed put.

I looked right into Tony's eyes and inside me a tree began to grow—a thick trunk like a

plumb line through my newly found body—
and my heart immediately stopped pounding.
We were alone in the world, our bodies pressed
tight together, locked in an iron grip. My stomach ached. His fist would leave an ugly bruise
and the collar of his jacket was digging into my
neck. I could feel an angry, burning red mark
being made.

But that was all.

There was no greed in his hands, no false
tenderness in his voice, no possessiveness in his
eyes. There was no sense that he wanted to get
at the softest part of me, what each person has
deep inside and must be treated with the utmost
care so as not to break. I wasn't playing a game
on someone else's terms. No, this was different,
something I'd never experienced before. It didn't
scare me. I understood it. The resistance in my
body melted away and Tony's grip loosened when
there was no longer anything hard to cling to. His
steely eyes glimmered with curiosity, but I calmly
pushed his body aside and gave him a nod to say
that I was ready. He didn't say anything. He just

reached out his big hands, let me put my muddy boot in his knitted fingers and gave me a leg up so I could climb through the window.

AGAIN AND AGAIN we played the new game. The lack of sleep crept in, a thin veil before my eyes that made the world swell gently. I enjoyed it. I wanted to stretch every minute, every second of this marvelous new reality.

I was the first one who snuck out to the greenhouse at night and the one who asked for just a little longer when the night started to turn into dawn. I was the one steering our steps toward the park, I was the one sweeping my gaze over the lawns, hunting for Tony's blunt silhouette, hoping he'd take us with him again.

Yes, this was my favorite game, but it wasn't long until I was playing it alone. Bella tired of it first. She reluctantly allowed us to convince her to come with us to the industrial zone. She didn't say much once we were there and one night she stopped in her tracks as we were nearing Tony's headquarters. "I'm done," she said. "They're idiots, I don't want anything to do with them."

Momo seemed a little lost, looking from me to Bella and then back at me. She liked having adventures in Tony's world. For her the boy-nights were one big lit-up theater stage. She enjoyed playing her role, she refined it until she knew it inside out and when morning came she crawled into her girl-bed with a happy sigh, filled with the experiences but happy to be home again.

Yes, for Momo it was a game, something she could do or do without, and she came with me a few more times. But one night after the Hawk started fiddling with some rolling papers, that was it for her. "Screw this, I'm out" she said, and from her expression I knew she thought I should do the same. I looked up at her, sensing Tony's shadow at my back.

"I'ma stay a while," I said. "Like another hour. Then I'll go."

Momo gave a curt nod. We both knew I was lying.

She left, and I stayed.

We never talked about it again, but the three of us knew that this was how it was going to be: Momo and Bella had chosen to go and I had chosen to stay. And when the leaden door shut behind Momo, Tony smiled. A crooked smile, but I could see what it meant: I was his now. My old life had nothing to do with me anymore.

TONY TOOK EVERYTHING, indiscriminately. Clothes, video games, cigarettes, liquor, mobile phones. Cars. Knives. Gasoline. Pills. Credit cards.

In the beginning he'd take both me and the Hawk with him. We took turns, one keeping watch and the other doing the raids. Tony stayed in the car and waited. The Hawk and I didn't say much while we worked, the air between us was quiet and charged. We knew it was a competition. When we returned with our spoils we glanced at our watches and everyone could see I was the fastest. After a few weeks the Hawk was left behind in the bunker. He didn't say anything about it but he had his back turned to us when we went on our way.

First it was one night every now and again,

then more and more often, sometimes several nights in a row.

It was Tony and me and the dark. He took me to parking structures, warehouses, backyards, office buildings. The first times he came with to stand guard, but then he left me on my own. Not before I came running and out of breath did he start the car. And only later, on the highway when he saw the spoils, was I allowed to feel the flash of his gaze on me. Just for a second, one critical second, and it didn't have anything to do with my body. His gaze said that I was *capable*, I was what he needed.

Yes, Tony tested me and discovered that I was good enough. It was never admiration, never friendship, just this: I had met the challenge he'd prepared for me. I measured up and he could imagine putting me through my paces me again, because it amused him to test my boundaries.

Why did I love that gaze? What gave rise to that hot billowing longing as soon as it washed over me? Maybe it was because no one had ever looked at me like that before. It goaded me. I knew I had to outdo myself each time in order to keep him. Each night was a battle with my own ability. I came back scratched and dog-bitten with burning lungs but never, neither before nor after, was I as powerful as I was then! And when we neared his headquarters sometimes he would stop and share the spoils with me. He sorted out what he thought was valuable enough, gave me half and threw the rest away, in the gutter or in the brush along the road. Wherever we'd been, we left a long wake of other people's possessions.

HE TOOK ME to a junkyard. It was at the edge of town next to a fallow field, we walked for a long time before we reached it. He didn't let me in on his plans, he never did, neither did I ask. It was a kind of protection, a necessary blindness: if I didn't know there was no risk of having second thoughts or being afraid. I let him lead me anywhere without hesitation.

It looked desolate in the dark. A gravel pitch surrounded by a high fence and behind the buildings were row after row of car roofs flashing in the shine of a few lone search beams. Tony walked along the ditch for a while before he made a decision, took off his shoes and threw them over the fence. He slipped his fingers into the metal mesh, climbed it like a cat. I was surprised how flexible he was, how that heavy compact body seemed suddenly weightless and limber.

I took off my shoes, tried to find a grip where Tony's hands had been, struggled to heave myself up. My feet slipped, then I realized that I was supposed to grip it with my toes. The thin metal threads cut into my sock and skin, and with a muffled moan I vaulted over, fell down in a heap on the other side. He was already over by the cars. A vague clinking could be heard and after that the neighing sound of the ignition turning over and over again without the motor starting. When I caught up with him he was doubled over in the front seat, shoulders pressed to the wheel and I could hear him swearing through his teeth. Then he sat up and tried again and gave a satisfied nod when the motor roared to life. It echoed between the buildings and instinctively I looked over my shoulder, but there was no one who could hear us. The junkyard was empty and silent.

He got out, left the car idling.

"You're driving."

A chill ran along my spine, palms sweating. Imagine him assuming I knew how and I'd have to tell him he was wrong! Everything he knew that I did not, all the knowledge he had that was inaccessible to me, it made me weak and unhappy. I was prepared to endure anything, but never his disappointment in me.

Tony sat on the passenger side. I clenched and opened my hands, closed and opened my mouth, trying to find words that could limit the damage as best they could, but before I got anything out, he leaned over and pounded the driver seat with his rough fist.

"Sit. I'll show you."

Whether he'd seen my worry or if I was the one who'd misunderstood, I didn't know. There was something unexpected in his voice, a friendly, encouraging tone. A flash below the brim of the cap, his eyes were in shadow but his mouth was relaxed, there was neither challenge nor hardness in it.

I sat. There was no key in the ignition, instead there was a little screwdriver. Tony bent over me, his face came close to mine, the hair under his hat smelled smoky and unwashed and I had to swallow hard so as not to miss what he said as he pointed and explained.

Gas on the right, clutch on the left, brake in the middle. Put it in one, release the clutch, easy on the gas.

The car jolted to a stop. My cheeks burned, I wanted to cool the hot skin with the back of my hand but I didn't, I didn't want him to notice. His voice was still gentle when he took hold of the screwdriver, turning it with a practiced twitch.

"Slower. You'll feel the bite point."

The car's frame rumbled softly beneath me. I tried to find my concentration again, gradually released my left foot. Then I understood what he meant. Tiny tremors went through the clutch pedal, getting stronger and stronger the higher I lifted my foot and I parried with my right foot, pressing the gas as slowly as I could. The motor surged and the car lurched forward, but it didn't stop. Tony's voice was eager, excited:

"Clutch down, now shift into two!"

I did as he said, feeling the wheels decouple for second before the gear's teeth took hold and the power increased. I thought about the moped boys at home, their screeching two-speed motors sputtering downhill. Their beloved DTs were tricycles compared to this.

I never wanted to stop. We drove round and round on the gravel pitch, Tony and I. Jumpstarting, backing up and slaloming between pickups and vans, until he suddenly pointed at the gates.

"Let's bust out."

I forgot myself, almost T-boning one of the parked cars and didn't think about what was coming out of my mouth.

"No!"

I can feel it in the air: how the corners of his mouth dropped in a contemptuous scowl. He stared out the window and for a second I thought his eyes would burn a hole right through me if he so much as looked my way. I gave it some gas, drove straight for the gates and slammed on the brakes just a few centimeters before the thick steel pipes.

"So open up."

He didn't smile, he said nothing, but I could see he was enjoying himself when he got out and searched his jacket pocket for something to pick the lock with. As we drove out of the junkyard I sped up, kept my eyes on the road when I asked why he hadn't opened the lock when we were trying to get in. He grinned.

"Those dumbshits spend a bunch of money on keeping people from getting in, but getting out is no problem."

The road ahead was empty and wide that night, my heart was pounding, the car felt yielding and natural in my hands. Then Tony grabbed hold of the steering wheel, pushed his foot on top of mine on the gas pedal. It hurt, the pain spread from my toes to my ankle and I gasped after breath:

"What the hell are you doing!"

The motor roared, the road turned, Tony tugged at the wheel but he didn't release the pressure on my foot, he just pushed harder, the speedometer rose steadily and then he whooped. He threw his head backward, howling like a wolf from deep down in his gut and then came the laughter, a gurgling insane laugh, as the car careened and the two right wheels lost their grip on the road, then slammed back down on the road.

My mind was rushing. He's insane, I thought, he's lost his mind, we're going to die. But his laughter filled the space and seemed to push inside me, I could feel his laughter in my body. The speed and the dark and the car's headlights on the asphalt, the blind forward propulsion, the excitement at the thought of death sitting on the roof and grinning, I couldn't keep it at bay and his laughter mixed with mine, hot blooded boy-laughter shrieking in the night.

Once we'd stopped, once we had driven off the asphalt road and onto a little side road, then we sat quietly in the car, breathless. There was a burnt smell, the car or maybe him, maybe it was his smell piercing my nostrils. When he reached out a hand and turned on the radio his arm came to rest on my thigh for second and my penis rose between my legs. Still so marvelous, that new, different throbbing that started up and spread through my body, making my nipples hard. I twisted in the seat, changing position so it wouldn't show. We sat there, listening to song after song, Tony drumming his thumb in time, and I was so happy. So fucking hopelessly, despairingly happy.

THE GREENHOUSE GLOWED in the sunset. The contours of the flower were like a shadow play inside the glass.

Momo and Bella were there when I arrived. Momo's arms were crossed, she was frowning at the flower. Concerned, Bella stroked the stalk, squeezing the fuzzy petals.

And I saw what they saw, but I didn't want to acknowledge it.

Eagerness swelled and writhed inside my delicate girl-body. Ahead of me was the view of yet another night filled with everything I could never get my fill of. Impatiently I fidgeted, craning my neck unintentionally. Momo eyes admonished me before she turned to Bella.

"What do you think?"

Bella gave Momo a worried look, then she looked back at the flower.

"She's not doing well. She needs to be left alone."

Momo didn't look particularly disappointed. She just nodded, walked out of the greenhouse, sat down on a folding chair and casually wagged her foot. Bella was pushing the flower's petals to the side and looking at the throng in there. I didn't consider how the question would sound.

"Is there any?"

Bella looked up from the flower, at me. Something dark flashed in her eyes, something I'd never seen before.

"Yes, there is. But you can't have any. She has to rest."

She turned away from me, reached for a spray bottle, and began misting the velvety petals.

SEVERAL TWILIGHTS LATER. Inside the glass walls of the greenhouse the flower-head hung on its stalk. She was sleeping, not to be disturbed.

My body was sitting in the middle of my girlhood room, but I wasn't there. My thoughts were full of night images, Tony's face, his back and hands, our excursions. I carried my boy-hours inside me like precious stones, each one brilliant, crystalline. I stored them behind my eyelids, under my skin, dragged them behind me on a string like a clattering, eye-catching toy.

I sat in my girl-room. Next to my bed was a mirror and each time I caught sight of my face I spent a second wondering who she was, that pale girl, before I remembered that she was me. Outside the moped boys did donuts in the gravel, and it was like some sort of incantation, a ritual being performed night after night. To ward off or to attract, which I didn't know. But I knew the boy in my girl-room wanted to be with them. He wanted to put on boots and shove his hands into his pockets, he wanted to greet them with a nod and stand with them in the gravel. But in the mirror was a girl's face, and she stared at me, dumb and not good enough, each time I met her gaze.

When darkness fell the walls had snuck so close that there was no longer space for me in the room.

I pushed walls and mirrors to the side, wriggling to the front door, pulling my boots on and walking outside. Quietly, I passed the boys and their mopeds. The motors were rushing, there was laughter and mumbling as I walked by. I kept my face turned away and my eyes steady on the glowing window—my goal—through which I could see Bella's silhouette.

That night we went out in our girl-bodies, Bella, Momo, and I.

I kept my head high and tried to feel a spring

in my step. I did the best I could. It wasn't fully dark, the blackbirds were still singing in the trees. The half-light and twilight were my armor now, maybe it would suffice.

It didn't.

I walked through the town in my girl-body and the gazes around me burned craters into my skin. I was seen by people, by children and dogs. In their pupils I was reflected and the reflection in the darkness of the eye was foreign to me. As though all of my girl-years, all the time I'd spent in that strange body, had been someone else's life.

Yes, I walked down city streets and I was carrying the girl-body like a shell, an oversized loden coat, an unshapely, ill-fitting masquerade costume.

The park was swarming with people. Momo walked slightly ahead of me and Bella. I could sense she was lost and worried, but for her it was different, it was a different kind of skew that chafed against her body. In among the crowds we went, in line after Momo. A few boys from our neighborhood were sitting there, I'd seen Momo talking to them. She made a beeline for them and suddenly we were sitting there, the three of us. A cigarette was being passed around but only Momo and I and one of the boys smoked it.

I don't remember what they talked about. But I remember Momo's natural laughter rising into the sky, how she let her body soften and be shaped by the boys' glances, the way she smiled at the blond, tanned one who'd handed her the cigarette. Seeing it made something shift strangely inside me. Disgust, and maybe jealousy. Bella sat in silence, her shyness didn't want to let go but her eyes were wide and curious. She was seeking attention from the awkward boys and when she caught it, she fluttered her lashes shut, smiled shyly looking down.

I looked out over the lawns. Cigarette cherries were glowing here and there. Laughter swelled and ebbed, music was crackling on a radio.

That's when he arrived.

I could feel it at my back, I knew he was there before I saw him, before I heard his voice. They sat down just a few meters away from us, behind and off to the side. I looked at Momo and Bella but they didn't notice anything, they were consumed with being seen.

Tony's legs were crossed as usual, he lit a cigarette and took a long drag so that the cherry sizzled. The girls laughed. Two doe-like girls. Long-legged and slender-necked, eyelids caked with makeup. One of them was on all fours like a dog, leaning toward Tony. Her loose sweater fell over one shoulder and his eyes slid over what he was seeing. His chest rose almost imperceptibly when he handed her the lighter she'd asked for. But then he looked away, ignoring her, indifferent to the fact that she was baring her white neck for him.

I twisted my stubby girl-fingers inside the arms of my sweater.

I asked the blond boy for a cigarette. He was dazed by Momo, but gave me one anyway. My legs tingled as I took those few steps over to Tony and asked him for a light.

I often wonder what would have happened if I'd stayed put. If I'd stayed with Bella and Momo and the others, or if I'd walked off, if I'd mumbled some sort of excuse and just got up and left.

But I did go over to Tony and asked for a light. He looked up, right at me, confused. No flicker of recognition in his eyes. He saw nothing familiar in my face, heard nothing familiar in my voice.

This didn't bother me.

But when I saw myself reflected in his pupils, when I saw what he saw!

In Tony's eyes my girl-body was loathsome, a piece of rancid meat not even fit to be scraps for the crows in the trees.

He didn't hand me his lighter. His face rearranged itself as a grimace and he did nothing to hide it. He wanted me to see. He held my gaze, making sure his disgust would slip inside me, so I would never forget that I was nothing to him.

Then he turned his head away. It took a moment before it occurred to me to turn my back to them. Tony said something, I didn't hear what, but I heard his tone, dripping with distaste. The doe-girls laughed softly but loud enough for me to hear.

Later that evening I lay in my girlhood bed.

The street lights painted a cold blue streak on the ceiling.

My chest felt empty and fit to burst, black and luminous white, silent and screaming. I put my hand over my face, looked at it in the dark. Let it glide across my stomach, in between my legs. The slit down there was dry, porous. My finger found the opening, found its way in, trying, suddenly desperately wishing that there would be some sensation, something of value. But there was nothing. It was dead, a mass of tissue without nerves or receptors.

It flickered behind my eyelids: Tony looking at me, me wearing my boy-body. He was looking at me and that was all. There was nothing else in his gaze.

I opened my eyes, sat up in bed. Longing crashed over me like a shock wave.

The light was on in Bella's room. I saw her shadow, she was bent over her notebook, writing with zeal. It wasn't like her, normally she only wrote short notes in her plant diary. She must have been writing about the boy, the awkward boy who'd made her smile and avert her eyes so shyly. I snuck along the rounded edge of the pool of light. When I reached the greenhouse I took off my boots, left them on the flagstones outside and tiptoed barefoot down the cement path. I thought I was just going to peek in, see how she was doing, if she'd perked up. She looked tired but healthy, the petals were elastic and their color clear and when I bent over to look at her sleeping head, the nectar sacs were bursting. It looked torturous. It made me think of boils, something infectious and poisonous. I touched them with my fingertips. Maybe it wasn't as Bella had said: it was best not to take any. She didn't know, she'd said herself that she'd never seen anything like it. She had no right to make such confident statements. Then I stopped thinking because my nail had punctured the thin membrane. Golden nectar flowed onto my finger. I felt her shudder, as though with relief, the pressure finally released.

TONY AND I were not alone in the bunker. The Hawk was there and he'd brought some people with him. A few boys I'd never met and two girls, eyes bright, lips wet with the alcohol that had been his treat.

We crowded on rock shelf down by the water. One of the girls was sitting right at the edge and the Hawk was sitting close to her, arm around her waist. She didn't brush his arm off, but I could tell she didn't like it, and was only allowing it so he'd keep sharing his bottle with her. He pressed his body to hers, pretending the rest of us were doing the pushing and his arm was all that was keeping her from tumbling over the edge, down into the water.

Tony sat across from them, the other girl beside him, and the Hawk kept stealing glances at the pair. I knew what he was thinking; she was his gift to Tony. The girl by Tony's side had the longest black eyelashes, the palest throat, and the reddest lips. She set her bottle on the rock and leaned into Tony, whispering something. He didn't reply, but I saw his mouth twitch. The Hawk noticed it too and winked theatrically, eager for contact and consensus from Tony.

Tony was indifferent to him.

He only had eyes for me.

I was squished between two strange boys, their heat, sweat and movements, but Tony's gaze was what was making my heart pound.

The girl beside him put her hand on his knee and ran her fingers along the seam of his jeans. The other hand found its way behind his back, up under his shirt. My eyes were fixed on his. In my peripheral vision, I saw her hands, how they were glued to him. It grossed me out. I wanted to rush over and shove her out of the way, tear away her sticky gaze and fingers. When I looked at Tony's face, I thought I noticed discomfort creeping under his skin, never mind the smile tugging at the corners of his mouth. He allowed her hand to make its way along his waist, he let her put her lips to his ear, but before she managed to say anything he got up. For a second her arm hung in midair, her hand pale and limp on the rock. Then it found the bottle in front of her, and she turned to one of the other boys.

Tony went to the cement door. The Hawk watched him go. He opened his mouth to speak, but then his girl bent over him, reaching for the bottle he'd placed out of reach and a wide gap opened up between her tank top and jeans, the stretch of white skin commanded the Hawk's full attention.

Tony expected me to follow him. I could tell by his movements, a sort of resoluteness I'd learned to recognize. When I caught up with him, he was standing in the bunker with his back to me, next to the armchair. The light from the door only reached a few meters into the room, but I could see him reaching down the seat and grabbing something. He stuffed it in his pants, then turned around. His jacket was open, the handle stuck up near his belly button. Matte black steel, hammer hidden by his waist band, barrel bulging at his fly.

He zipped his jacket up, the handle concealed but the outline of the barrel apparent.

"Let's get out of here."

I nodded. Anything could happen next, but I nodded anyway. In my pockets, my fists were trembling, but not for one second did I think of turning back.

He took me past the industrial zone. Large desolate plots, untouched in anticipation of additional factories, additional warehouses being built. All there was so far was a row of streetlamps standing at attention between the fields. They were unlit; it was still light out that summer night. The grass grew poorly, the ground was earthy and dark. In the distance was the hum of the highway, but around me it was so quiet I could hear my own breathing.

Tony was standing by the derelict fence. Most of the posts were leaning but a few were upright, three in a row like soldiers standing at attention.

He picked a few rusty cans off the ground and placed them on the posts. I closed one eye, then the other. How far was it? Ten meters?

He came back, brushing his hands off on his jeans. I could see the weapon under the wristlet of his jacket. Then he bent down and ran his practiced hands over the earth, found a slender rope. When he pulled it, it rose like a snake from the dust. He pointed at the cans.

"Fifteen meters."

He held out the weapon, nodding at me to take it. I looked at the black handle, the loose-seeming hammer, at Tony. The glint in his eyes made me feel transparent, as though my awkwardness was cracking open and loosening my boy-skin. I wanted to grab hold of the pistol, fire it, and nail all three cans as though I'd done many times before. But in my mind I could see myself slipping, fumbling, losing grip.

Tony grinned at my hesitance.

"First time?"

I nodded. His grin widened, as though my insecurity was making the game more fun. His hand gestured quickly. He held the weapon with both hands, stretching out his arms and after that came the bangs, three in a row. The sound almost made me fall backward. It echoed over the field and the pain hit my ears before I had a chance to cover them. I looked up to see one can still on a post. The other two were on the dusty ground.

He didn't ask if I wanted to, it wasn't for me to decide. He reloaded the gun, showed me the safety, how you pulled it back until it clicked. Hands clasped around the handle, index finger resting on the trigger as you aimed, the sight in line with the muzzle.

I stood there with the weapon, testing the trigger with my finger. There was tension, resistance. As I aimed, the sight shook.

My ears were still ringing after Tony's shots and I wanted to shoot and yet I didn't want to, I wanted to know how it felt and yet I didn't. Everything that had happened, everything I'd done those nights with Tony, it had been a wild game. Until this moment my boy-body had made me feel immortal, like a superhero costume that enabled me to do impossible things. It was a shell from which every scratch and bruise faded as I slept. But this was something else. I was holding a loaded gun with real bullets, and while I tried to sharpen my gaze I thought about a bullet to the heart, a pulse that stopped pounding, lungs that stopped breathing—not something that could fade and disappear. A dead body is a dead body, no matter how immortal it might seem.

I lowered my arms.

"I can't see. It's too dark."

Tony squinted at the cans. He was having a hard time focusing. For second I thought he was going to agree with me, the muscles in his neck tensed as though he were about to nod. Then one of the streetlights by the fence flickered. A red flash, then darkness, like an electrical glitch before a short. But then the lamps lit up, one by one. The contours of the tin can sharpened, soon it was bathed in light.

I didn't need to be facing Tony, my entire back could sense him grinning, expecting me to shoot and miss.

This, his wordless ability to challenge me, him hoping I would fail and succeed in equal parts, it made me dizzy. His eyes were glued between my shoulder blades, the anticipation in his grin, it spread across my skin like an armor and my hands steadied, beyond the sight was the can.

I pulled the trigger.

My arms flew up with the recoil and I stumbled backward, regained my balance and lowered my hands. My fingers had stiffened around the handle, seemed to want to merge with the weapon.

Never had I felt such power!

I looked up. Three empty posts.

I didn't turn around, I spoke right out into the air:

"Line them back up."

No answer. I couldn't tell if he was moving or still, but I could feel his surprise. I prepared myself for a blow to the back of the head or a half nelson.

Out of the corner of my eye, I saw him walk toward the fence in the dark. His back was a moving target.

I stood there, weapon lowered, barrel pointed at the ground, and wondered what was moving through his mind. I'd given him an order and he'd obeyed. His back was to me and I was holding his gun. I didn't know how to read it, didn't know what it meant. For a few seconds I thought the balance between us was in flux. But when he turned around, everything was back to normal. I could tell by his posture, his steps, his expression even though I could hardly make out his eyes in the dark. There was no worry, no suspicion. In a flash I remembered something I'd heard about wolves: only a male who was sure of his position of power could afford to turn his back.

The cans were up. Tony was beside me again.

"Do we need to reload?"

He shook his head.

"You have four shots left."

I raised my hands, aimed, and tested the trigger. Just as I was about to fire I heard Tony's voice, close to my ear:

"First the left, then the right, then the middle one."

I nodded. Suddenly it felt simple, natural. The weapon became an extension of my hands and when I shot my inner eye saw the can fall before it actually did. It was like someone had stretched a thin string between the muzzle of the gun and the cans. The bullet flew straight and true, hitting right where I wanted it to. The left can, the right, then the middle one—I hit all three. Tony sucked air through his teeth, making a low, surprised sound.

"First time, huh?"

I nodded.

"I have one shot left, line them up again."

He looked at me. There was no trace of the appreciation I'd just seen, his eyes narrowed, his jaw set. The tingle moved through me, fear or curiosity. I had become reckless, gone too far, crossed the thin line he allowed me to near.

He reached out his hand. I held his gaze and gave him the gun. He took it without breaking eye contact, slipped his finger around the trigger as he spoke.

"The last shot is mine."

Slowly he raised his hand, slowly he pointed the barrel at my chest. I didn't blink, I could feel my eyes burning as I tried to hold back the fear trying to push its way out. Then Tony raised the gun even higher, pointing it at his own head.

"An empty magazine is worth nothing when everything goes to hell."

He put the gun to his temple.

"In movies people shoot themselves in the head, that's bullshit. If you want to kill yourself, shoot yourself in the mouth. Up and at an angle, toward the roof of your mouth. Then all you have to do is squeeze."

And that's what he did. He put the barrel in his mouth, his finger on the trigger. Something murky crept into his eyes, he was looking at me and yet not, his lips were a pale red O around the black metal.

I tried to inhale but there was no room, my lungs felt pinched. When I looked at him with the barrel in his mouth, when I saw that even he

didn't know what was going to happen next—
I've never been so afraid for anyone, never loved
anyone as much as I had in that moment.

Then he let the barrel slide out of his mouth.
It was shiny, wet with saliva. He licked his lips, like
after a delicate meal. I didn't know what was written on my face in that moment, but when Tony
looked back at me he started laughing. A warm
laugh, almost brotherly. For second I thought he
was going to pat me on the shoulder, but he just
turned around and walked off across the field.

TIME PASSED. A few days, at most a week, but longer than usual between contact, between Bella, Momo, and me. They didn't come to my window and I didn't go to theirs.

They were probably seeing each other, surely they were sitting in Momo's room or Bella's garden as usual, maybe they were talking about me. I didn't really think about which it was, because I was busy dragging myself through the daylight hours. In the day, reality was sort of blurred, like I was nearsighted and had forgotten to wear my glasses.

Then afternoon came. I slept in my girlhood bed, an exhausted sleep after a long night. Wild dreams raged deep inside me, everyday sounds and waking life were blocked from my senses. The phone rang and rang, it took a long time before it cut into my dreams I woke up because my dad was at my door.

"Are you awake? It's Bella."

I sat up and in my sleep-drunkenness I forgot that my upper body was that of a teenage girl. I yanked the blanket up, catching his embarrassed expression before he made his way back out the door. I picked up the phone, surprised at the brittleness in my voice.

"Hello?"

Her voice was sharp.

"You have to get over here. Now, right away."

Momo was standing outside the greenhouse. She was looking at me through her bangs when I arrived, digging the toe of her shoe into the seam between the stone slabs. Inside the glass wall Bella was kneeling by the stalk. She was digging her fingers into the ground at the foot of the stem, feeling the root threads and knobs. When I came in she signaled for me to come closer.

"Look here."

I shuffled across the cement path. My legs

resisted, and I didn't dare look at her because I sensed it, I knew. Bella pointed at one of the knobs of the root.

"Touch it."

I crouched down next to her and touched the earthy clump. It was spongy, yielding like a rotten fruit. Bella could tell I could feel it too, and nodded slowly.

"She's rotting. From the inside."

I put my hand to her sick body and looked at the black earth. Bella's voice was as serious as a grown-up:

"In time she's supposed to drop her petals, wither, and shrink. But she's not supposed to *rot*.

Then she looked up, fixed her gaze on mine:

"Kim, why is she rotting?"

I glimpsed Momo in my peripheral vision. She was in the doorway waiting for me to say something, but there was no hard aura around her, no angry red cheeks. I faced her when I replied:

"How am I supposed to know?"

But Momo looked at the ground.

Bella got up, hands on her hips.

"Oh come on. You've been here, you've tapped her nectar. Even though you know she's weak."

I got up too, but I couldn't look her in the eye. I turned back to Momo, opening my hands, trying to get the indignation in my voice to sound authentic:

"Tell her she's wrong!"

Momo's voice was brittle, not powerful and resounding as usual.

"I don't think so, Kim. I don't think we're wrong."

The morning sun shimmered on the glass walls, the insects buzzed gently, sweet smells and humid heat rose from the flowerbeds.

I looked at them, they stood there in the greenery, between them and me was a line.

Bella, Momo.

And me.

I shrugged.

"Believe what you want. I don't know what the hell you're talking about.

So I turned my back to Bella and the flower. My shoulder checked Momo's, she lost her balance and had to catch her breath. Bella's voice hit my back like a handful of small nails.

"You're *messed up!*"

I didn't turn around, but I hocked a slimy loogie into her red flower bed before I walked out the gate.

THAT NIGHT I took my boots off at the edge of Bella's garden. Barefoot and like a small child I tiptoed across the flagstones, and when I reached the greenhouse there was a lock on the door. It was substantial, the bolt was sturdy, the key was probably thick. I couldn't help but smile at it, a smile so wide it ached.

I found a bit of metal wire in my jacket pocket, my hands set to work of their own accord, I didn't need to think. It clicked, the bolt slid out. I opened the flimsy door, leaving no footprints on the cement path as I walked in.

Little Bella. She thought thick metal and a sturdy lock was enough to keep me out. But the Kim she had known, the girl who'd been her friend and playmate, wasn't the same Kim who was greedily bending over the flower's head.

THE SUMMER NIGHT was cool, the river clucked against the rock slabs. Tony slithered down the large boulders, slipping a little where it was wet. I followed him.

Down by the water was a flat rock, big enough for two to stand on. Tony looked at the water. He grabbed the hem of his sweater and pulled it and T-shirt over his head. He tugged off his untied boots, put his hand on the buttons of his fly, eagerly unbuttoning them one by one. With a single movement he pulled off his jeans and underpants and socks and left them like a molted skin on the rocks. His muscles, the tight white buttocks as he leapt straight into the dark, the way he blinked the water from his eyes when he resurfaced.

My bodily memories tussled with each other. My hands hesitated, unsure of what was hiding beneath my clothes, but then I looked at Tony. Boyishness lit up his eyes, and suddenly I remembered who I was. I tore off my clothes.

The water was silky. It embraced me, parting to receive my weight. When I resurfaced he was gone. I looked around. No rings, no bubbles. In the distance I heard the monotonous thump of the shipyard. The river suddenly seemed deep and black. I took a few random strokes but then was left treading water.

I saw no shadow, felt no swells when he arrived. He wrapped his arms around my waist and pulled, gliding up, his skin to my skin, pressing me beneath the surface, holding me down.

I wasn't afraid. I opened my eyes to his body in the inky night water. The stomach muscles, the rivulet of hair below his belly button. The strong hips, the smooth groin and the curly carpet of pubic hair, the soft wrinkly dick swaying in the water. I kept my eyes wide open. The water stung but I wanted to keep looking, I wanted to burn the image on my retina. But after a while the air in my lungs was almost spent and I twisted, kicking to get out of his grip. He held me down. His hands were forceps, they clamped to my arms, my shoulders, my neck, and my throat cramped. Now it was flashing before my eyes and fear shot through my body. This is death, I thought. Here it is, this is what it's like.

But Tony gave in. He was still gripping my neck, maybe he was pulling me up before letting go. My head was above the surface, I drew a greedy breath, gasping, coughing. The water was carrying me. I was on my back, I was alive. My vision flared and my throat ached but the feeling of oxygen spreading through my body, the feeling of life!

Tony didn't say anything, letting me catch my breath. He turned away and swam slowly out into the middle of the river, his shoulder blades luminous at the surface.

He waited.

I dove, swimming in a circle around him. He was kicking lazily when I came close, but when I grabbed him around the chest he jerked, stiffened. I pushed him under the surface, did what he'd done: climbed up his body until I was on top. At first he didn't struggle. His body was bigger than mine, it wanted to float up like a buoy but he was helping, we held him down with our mutual strength. He took short shallow strokes and I moved my weight across him, balancing us both against the buoyancy of the water.

Many seconds passed before his muscles seized up. First there were tiny movements, involuntary, instinctive. An arm shot up. I grabbed it, pushed it down. He twisted. I held on. He scrabbled, the movements becoming more and more jerky. I felt the panic in his body and the adrenaline that came rushing. My muscles filled with new power, and suddenly I longed to feel his lifeless body in my hands. That strength of his, that damned boy-strength and that body and the silence, I couldn't stand it. I couldn't stand his skin and his hands, I couldn't stand his coolness, that he couldn't feel what I felt.

And this was all I would ever get.

I pushed him down.

He softened. I was still holding on, my muscles had locked. But Tony's body was limp now, his throat had relaxed. A chill ran down my spine. I let go, unsure of whether I wanted to see him dead or alive.

He shot up like a projectile. I was thrown backward and my head sank below the surface for a second. When I came up again he was on his back a little ways away in the water. He was laughing. Loud, rowdy laughter, whooping, drawing deep breaths between the gasps.

He'd tricked me. The devil had tricked me.

I could feel the lactic acid coursing through my limbs. The water kept me afloat, after the lactic acid came the endorphins. Tony's laughter echoed between the rocks and suddenly I was laughing too. It was the madness that had rolled in over him, it was so hopelessly contagious. It should have frightened me, frightened me off. I should have gotten out of there and never come back but I couldn't, I wanted to be inside his madness, I wanted to feel it, I wanted to be within the radius of its limitless power.

He dove. I closed my eyes, waiting for his hard arms to wrap around my waist.

SOMETIMES MY PARENTS asked after Momo and Bella. Cautiously, in passing: Did anything happen, had we stopped being friends? I shrugged and said it was nothing special, we weren't not friends, but like, we didn't have that much in common anymore. They looked a little worried but all they did was pat me awkwardly on the cheek. Their worry came with an equal measure of hope, like they were sighing with relief when they realized that I'd left the masquerade games of childhood behind. "She's normal after all," they thought. "Better late than never, but now we can be sure: our daughter is normal. She's developing just as she should."

No, my parents weren't particularly concerned that their daughter had dark rings under her eyes and was barely responsive before sometime in the afternoon. Not until much later, one night when they were awakened by raspy shrieks and the sound of glass being crushed, only then did they open their eyes for a second, sensing that something had happened to their child.

WE WERE DRIVING in a car.

There was a burning smell, Tony had pushed the speedometer way past the two-hundred mark. When the blue light appeared he drove farther and farther into the forest, gravel was spraying from the tires, and my eyes were glued to the rearview mirror, hands clamped to the seat, and I was thinking: "They're gonna get us, this time they're gonna get us, and then . . ."

Finally, we stopped with a jolt and it was silent. No cars, no sirens, just a faint hush through the fir trees. I sat still for a long time, feeling my pulse pound through my body but I didn't want to move, didn't want to scream, I wanted to sit there and feel my tingling limbs.

Tony was sitting still, too, eyes shut. A thick blue vein was pulsing at his throat, quickly at first and then more slowly. He opened his eyes. They were calm and clear and he reached for the cigarettes, took one out for each of us. The window had fogged with our breath and body heat. I rolled the window down, the oxygen-rich night air rolled in and mingled with the smoke. Tony climbed out, took a lap around the car, and leaned in through my window.

"It's stuck. Really fucking stuck."

He laughed. I grinned.

"What should we do?"

He stood up straight, took a drag, blew the smoke at the night sky.

"Hitchhike."

And I gave a heavy sigh and was about to say that the last thing I wanted to do right now was hitchhike, in the middle of the night, when he opened the trunk and folded down the back seats. I twisted in the front seat, watched him crawl in. He could almost lie down flat.

"Are we going to sleep *here*?"

He didn't reply. He just lay there, with his jacket crumpled under his head. Next to him was space for another body. For me.

I crawled over the seats. I laid on my back, staring at the ceiling of the car, not daring to look at Tony. I was afraid. Of being caught by the police, of falling asleep, of not getting home before my parents woke up.

And most of all of Tony, because he was lying there. So close to me.

After a while he fell asleep. His breathing changed, not calmer but deeper, like he was having a hard time getting air. I cautiously turned my head. He was facing me with his hand by his mouth. He was already dreaming, his eyelids twitched, there was a deep groove between his eyebrows. A sound escaped. A brief feeble hoarse grumble, not much more than an exhalation. My hand hesitated, hung in the air. I wanted to touch him, put my hand to his head—there was nothing I was more afraid of doing.

His throat trembled as he took a long, uneasy breath. Hot air streamed toward me.

I put my boy-hand to his cheek.

He grabbed it in his sleep, pressed my hand to his boy-mouth, breathed into it. Carefully, I caressed his face, touching his stubby chin, stroking my thumb over his tense temple. His eyelids smoothed out, his throat relaxed. His body shifted into sleep breathing.

We lay like that.

A large bird rose up, it was so close, I heard its heavy wings beating.

A badger or a wild boar was rummaging around outside, grunting a little, waddling away.

The night turned blue, paled.

We lay like that.

His cheek in my hand, his wet hot breath against my skin. I didn't shut my eyes for one second. I kept my eyes wide open, storing each second of his slumber in my palm.

Not before the gray dawn started creeping in through the window did I take my hand back. I crept out of the car, moving as silently as I could until I reached the asphalt road and could start hitchhiking.

IT WAS A high summer night, the ground was still warm from the sun. The Hawk and I were at the edge of the forest. Tony was boosting a car. I had brought tools. The Hawk's hands were in his pockets. There have to be three of us, Tony had said, and the Hawk had jumped up from the floor so quickly I almost thought he'd click his heels and salute.

Tony took a while. The tools weighed down my shoulders and we had nothing to say to each other. I put my backpack aside and kept an eye on the road in the direction of where the car was supposed to turn up. The Hawk was whistling a little between his teeth. Then he turned to face the forest, searching for the zipper of his fly. I glimpsed his white wrinkly dick, the stream of piss hitting the tree trunk glittered in the evening sun. My backpack was too close, it got sprayed with a few drops and I wanted to move it but I let it be, I didn't want to give him the satisfaction. He peed slowly, rocking on his heels. Then he started talking, eagerly, as though he were in a rush to have said what he wanted to say. It was about Tony and a girl he'd fucked. Her porn star moans, how she had screamed and begged for his cum in her mouth. And Tony had sprayed her face with it and then, once he'd pulled up his pants, he'd taken out a one hundred kronor bill and stuck it to the sperm on her cheek. "Here you go, you fucking whore," he'd said, and then left.

There was such strange pride in his voice. He kept his eyes on the stream of piss until he finished talking and winked at me under his thick bangs.

I tried to imagine it. Tony with the girl, him fishing a bill out of his pocket and smacking it to her sticky cheek. But I couldn't, I couldn't conjure the image. I couldn't see him doing that. It seemed so unlike him, so studied and over-the-top. Tony didn't need to go that far to annihilate someone, all he had to do was look at you with that steely gaze of his. No, the Hawk was lying.

Telling a tale, a myth he'd spun about his master. I didn't say anything, kept my poker face up and my eyes on the bend in the road. The Hawk chuckled, batted away the last drops and put his dick back in his pants. The smell of hot piss rose from the earthy forest floor. He faced me.

"What about you, Kim? You haven't fucked anyone? A girl, I mean."

I looked at him. At his watery pig eyes and the expectant grin he couldn't hide. I should have been afraid of him. He hated me because I was Tony's new apprentice and I knew he always had a stiletto knife on him. But I wasn't afraid, I couldn't be. His grin, the way he thought he'd found out my secret, and finally had the upper hand. I felt sorry for him. His body was overflowing with fat, his fingers were clumsy, he had no imagination. Once he'd been in Tony's grace but I'd replaced him. He had nothing, his world had crumbled. I was about to tell him he was right, I'd never fucked a girl, but then we heard the sound of an engine coming down the road and Tony pulled to a stop in front of us.

ONE NIGHT I fell asleep early. I'd spent several nights in a row with Tony and needed to sleep in. But I woke up again, with a jerk. My girl-ears had heard something, familiar sounds pushing sleep aside. Clattering, laughter, music. Soft, soft I heard it in the silence of the terraced-house night, like mice under a blanket of leaves.

I crept out of bed and quietly opened the window. From the living room I heard a muted mumble from the television. I dropped my boots out the window and they landed with silent thud on the grass. I climbed out and tiptoed beyond earshot of my parents before I pulled the boots on. I followed the seam between the sidewalk and the gutter, followed the tinkling sound. I knew what I was hearing, I'd known from the start but refused to believe it, wishing childishly and blue-eyed that the sound would turn out to be something else.

They were sitting outside the greenhouse. The soft yellow flames flickered over their girl-bodies, over hand mirrors, over the powder compacts, over their masked faces: red lips, blackened lashes, cheeks stained with rouge. Momo stood behind Bella, braiding her hair—the textured unruly red swell ran between her fingers—shaping it, taming it with a brush and band. Bella held up a mirror to her face and made mirror-faces at herself: preening, flirting, admiring the painted girl she saw.

Momo and Bella were having a masquerade. They were playing a game. Their voices came flying at me like sparks: outsized, delighted. The greenhouse door was open, inside the flower head was nodding but they didn't give her so much as a glance. They were consumed with their new mirror images, their new masks.

I was on the other side of the garden hedge, the dark leathery leaves turned the picture before me into a puzzle. I saw their painted faces, the insurmountable line between them and me, and the sorrow that came flooding. The games, our games, our bodies in unison. It was lost, I had absented myself. I ached, my body yearned for the togetherness they had over on the other side, but to have a face like that, to become, to be—I could never play that game. I could never follow them down that path.

TONY AND I were running through the forest. I still had my tools on me; on the highway, the sirens were wailing, but we were almost
there. They had no chance of catching us, not this
time either. I outdid myself: I'd shut off the alarm,
gotten in and out in under a minute. Tony had
hitched himself up and helped pull me out of
the cramped opening and when I fell down onto
the ground his cautious grip was around my arm.
He pulled me to my feet, gently shoved my back,
and then we ran, Tony first, his backpack like an
unshapely hunchback. The pine needles flew up
from our speeding feet. Dodging and ducking the
thick branches, I had no problem keeping up. I
ran right behind him and heard the thudding of
his boots on the ground, I heard his heavy breaths,
his chest bursting with life, and I widened my
gait, wanting to be running even closer to him,

and then we fell. Our feet tangled together and we tumbled over the tussocks like two bear cubs, clambering to each other and rolling around. His face was so close, so close and his spit showered my cheeks. We both wailed with laughter and pain, and I ended up on the bottom.

Tony lay on top of me, his heavy body heaving with breath. He straddled me, hands clamped to my wrists, and his erection against my thigh. Tony was a weight on top of me, he pinned me to the moss. I could tell he was surprised.

He knew what I was feeling.

His dick was throbbing, and he knew I could feel it. And there, in the dark forest on the soft pine needle carpet, I could've opened up a new reality, I could've taken Tony's head in my hands, I could've kissed him with my boy-lips, I could have whispered to him that it could be like this, we were allowed, and it *should* be like this, there was nothing to be afraid of. I could've wrapped my strong arms around his torso, taken a wrestling hold around his waist, held him fast and said the words again and again until he understood: Love exists,

Tony. I have love to give you. You're searching for death but it's love you're longing for, I know it, I've seen it. Let's stop this game, all of your love is here, inside me, I have more than enough.

I could've held him there, held him all night long, encouraged him to explore my boy-body. Forced him to stay long enough to see my other self.

But I didn't do anything and a gap in reality widened. Tony recoiled like he'd burned himself, rearranging his hoodie, which was twisted around his chest. A strange fear lit up his face. He snorted like an animal before he started running. Taking long strides, his arms pumping at his sides with full power, like he wanted to run away from himself.

For one short, magical moment there had been a possibility. Now it was gone.

I got up, felt my wet seat. Felt my dick shrink with the cold, let the damp chill wash away all the heat. Then I ran after him, outran him, ran until the ground was but a blur beneath my feet.

AFTER THAT NIGHT Tony didn't look me in the eyes anymore.

When I'd arrive he'd lift his chin in greeting as usual but his eyes were fixed in the distance, over my head or looking right through me.

Yes, Tony refused to look at me and without his gaze I started to crumble. When the barking dogs and wailing sirens neared, when the moment arrived and Tony was tramping outside the opening in the wall, I shut down. It was like something froze. My heart stopped pounding, but it wasn't calm that was spreading. I just stood there clutching the spoils. Tony had to drag me through the warehouse door, pull my body through the gap in the fence so the dogs wouldn't get me.

DAWN WAS ON the horizon. I was heading home.

My wrists ached, purplish marks had appeared
where he'd grabbed me with his large fists. His
hand came flying once we were shielded by the
trees. The dogs sniffed around but kept to the
fence and I heard their distant barking as Tony's
palm slapped my cheek, flinging my head to the
side and strewing stars behind my eyelids. I kept
my eyes closed, his muffled voice was like a chill
against my face.

"I should have let them get you."

I didn't reply, but I put the back of my own
cool hand against the burning skin.

I walked in between the townhouses, my window
was ajar just as I had left it. For the first time in a
long time, I wanted to be in there. I wanted to hide

I STAYED IN my girlhood room for a few nights. When twilight fell, it tore and tugged at my body, but I didn't know where to go. There didn't seem to be a single body left that fit me.

Then dawn arrived.

I quickened through my dreams and woke with a start. The room's edges were dust-gray in the early morning. My stomach ached; it was what woke me. Below my belly button a tingle, a new but not unknown pain. I flew out of bed, stars danced before my eyes as the blood rushed down through my body.

The strip light in the bathroom was sharp and white. Overhead, I could hear one of my parents turning over heavily in their bed. I crouched on the cool plastic floor, cupping my hand between my legs. A long blackish string of mucus: like webbing between my fingers. I tore off a piece of toilet paper, wiped hard, rubbing between my legs. The paper was full of rusty lumps. An inevitable viscous mark of time.

I ran across the asphalt barefoot. The seam of my pajama pants absorbed the wet red rust and the pain in my tummy struck me with each step. The gravel dug deep into the soles of my feet, the sunrise was a pale pink veil across the sky. I ran, hands pressed to my belly, overflowing with tears, the salt stiffened on my cheeks. All I saw was the asphalt and the sun's fiery tongue lapping the greenhouse walls. It was like an orange grid shining amidst all the damp, gray morning. In there her tired head was nodding and when I saw it a loud whimper escaped me: the withered petals bent toward the ground, awaiting death.

She gave a little shake, as though she were trying to look at me. I held her head, raised the opening in the petals to my face. The crown of the flower was heavy. When I stuck my nail in the nectar sac, the long stalk twitched almost imperceptibly. I whispered, stroked her clumsily with my free hand as the nectar seeped over my finger: "I'm sorry, I'm sorry about this but without it I can't live."

I could hardly wait until the nectar sac was emptied of its contents. I stuck my finger in my mouth but it wasn't enough. My entire body was screaming for more. I pierced another sac and then another, greedily sucking down the sweetness until I felt the familiar jolt. I didn't need to seek out my reflection in the glass walls, I could feel the change in every cell. My hand found its way between my legs, eagerly feeling around inside the pants. There were balls and a penis. No cleft, no hole to bleed through.

I crouched down, cupped my head in my boy-hands, rocking back and forth. Guilt pounded behind my eyelids. I opened my eyes wide, saw my reflection in the glass. It was an empty boy-face, there was no sparkle in his eyes anymore.

The sun was burning by the time I woke up. Quietly, I got up, the skin of my thighs tight with dried blood and I felt between my legs. The flow had stopped. Nothing more was running out of me.

On the street a car was starting, through the hedge some children were playing on the sidewalk. I was in my pajamas in a greenhouse. My hair was sweaty and my feet were bare and black with dirt. I rested my forehead on the glass, snorted with despairing laughter. It was all madness.

In the stifling greenhouse, an eternity passed by before Bella found me. She'd come from the house, putting on her gardening gloves as she walked. She flung open the greenhouse door. She cried out when she caught sight of me, then pushed me aside and focused her attention on the flower. Her head was bowed deeply, asleep perhaps. Bella grabbed her forehead.

"How many did you take?"

I didn't answer and she looked into the flower, drawing a breath when she saw all the empty nectar sacs. Then she grabbed me hard by the arm, pushed me out through the glass door.

I stumbled onto the flagstones and stood there as she examined the flower. She mixed a small bottle of plant food, and watchfully sprayed the earth and petals. When she emerged she shoved me in the direction of the house. I walked with my head down, she with her eyes flashing black.

I washed myself in her bathroom, tried to scrub my feet clean but dark flecks remained where the gravel had dug in. Bella didn't knock, she just opened the door and tossed in a pile of clothes, closing the door before I could say "Thank you." By the time I came out she was at the kitchen table. It rustled as I walked. Her clothes were too big for me, the belt made the waistband bunch up. I sat down in the chair across from her, one foot up on the seat.

"How is she doing?"

The rage lingered in Bella's eyes but was weaker now, fatigued.

"She's alive. Barely."

She buried her face in her hands.

"You could have killed her. You're stealing

her strength and you don't even care, as long as you get your kicks."

Her jaw was tense, her red curls swung as she shook her head, resigned.

"It's enough now, Kim. I just can't anymore."

I looked at her face, at her soft breasts under her T-shirt. She was becoming a woman, she would grow into and live with a woman's body.

How could she want this, *choose* this!

I couldn't wrap my head around it.

She raised her eyebrows.

"Did you hear me?"

I squeezed my fists, nails digging into my palms.

"You're throwing your life away, Bella."

She snorted.

"Me? *I'm* the one who . . ."

I didn't let her finish. I jumped to my feet, talking over her.

"Did you forget what it's like, what they do to people like us? Have you forgotten? Because it will never be any different, no matter how old we get. Not if you look like this."

I made a gesture that took in my entire girl-body. Bella sat in silence for a second. On the table, the botany book was open and she was stroking the color pictures, running her finger over seedpods and petals and root threads when she finally replied.

"I haven't forgotten."

She looked up at me.

"But I'm not going to hate myself just because they do. I don't intend to let them win."

I shut my eyes. From there, I could see this from Bella's perspective, I could see myself standing in the kitchen. And I understood: you couldn't see it from the outside. She couldn't understand it, but the Kim that was visible to her didn't exist anymore. She was seeing the shell of a body, but she wasn't seeing me. I heard her get up and walk around the room as she talked.

"I've spoken with the botanical institute. They're coming to collect her. The arrangements have been made."

I opened my eyes, and broke out in a panicked sweat at my hairline.

"What did you tell them?"

"I told them she's special, but they don't know what she can do yet."

"When will they be here?"

Bella bit her lip.

"Soon, they said. So any day now, I guess."

THAT NIGHT I sat in my girlhood room with my eyes closed and my hands covering my ears. I was trying to block out the shouting but it pushed its way in, seeping between my fingers and hammering wedges under my eyelids. From the city and the streets and the harbor came the shouting, and from the greenhouse and my reflection and from inside, too, from my cells. The word *soon* was like a noose around my neck tightening with each passing minute. Beyond the moment of choking was no self, no Kim, nothing. Just some sort of unalive state.

I wandered the darkened neighborhood, aimlessly following the footpaths. Beyond Bella's garden hedge lay the greenhouse. Memories moved through my mind:

Tony and me in the trunk of the car, his face

in my hand. He opens his eyes, he looks down at a face, into a pair of eyes. The face is a girl's, but the eyes are mine.

THE LIGHTS WERE off at Momo's house but behind the frosted bathroom window glass it shimmered, the glimpse of a slim shadow inside. The shadow jumped when I knocked but when I waved, she opened up and stuck her head out, toothbrush in mouth. She stopped brushing when she caught sight of me, hissing out of the corners of her mouth. Toothpaste dribbled down her chin.

"What is it, what are you doing?"

"I have to do it one more time, Momo. One last time."

Momo's eyes wavered. She pulled her head in and I heard her spit before she popped her head back out.

"What are you thinking of doing?"

I threw open my hands, took in my entire lanky girl-body in the space between my palms.

"Show him that I can be transformed. Into this."

Momo's eyes opened wide.

"You're nuts!"

She leaned over, almost falling out the window, stuttering:

"You'll never, he'll never, that would be . . ."

I raised my voice until it drowned out hers.

"I know. That's why I'm telling you. You have to promise to look for me if I don't come back."

I stared at the gray pavement along the house.

"Check in with her in a little while. And tell her she has to forgive me."

Then I turned my back to the illuminated square and walked toward the greenhouse. Behind me, I heard Momo shut her window.

I STOPPED THE car at the edge of the industrial zone. After the engine had quieted down my breathing was all that was audible, aside from the soft creaking of leather whenever I moved in the seat. I ran a finger over the cool, rare hardwood instrument panels. I could picture it clearly: how his eyes would open wide when he saw it, his eagerness to drive on the highway and push the pedal to the metal, how I'd be sitting beside him breathless with speed and excitement until we were too far away from the city to turn back. I smiled to myself and felt a sting of playfulness. This is a kidnapping, I thought, this body is my camouflage and the car is my bait.

Yes, that's how I imagined it. I would steal his attention, lure him away, bribe him with the promise of speed and danger. I would lead him far away, to a place where we could be until he'd seen me for who I was.

He was on the outcrop when I arrived, a familiar silhouette against the water and sky. Something was going on. They'd made a fire, bottles and cans were strewn around them. By the stream at the edge of the forest I could make out a few others, it seemed to be mostly boys and a few girls. They were stumbling around in the trees, their shouts echoing. The Hawk's shadow freed itself from the dark. As he came closer I saw that he had a gleaming white beer can in his hand and that his sweater sleeve was wet up to his elbow. He raised the beer can in the air.

"What the hell are you doing here, you fuckin' pussy? Nobody invited you."

He glanced at the stream at the edge of the forest, where girls were stumbling around. They were wearing slim high heels, their high-pitched voices shrieked with laughter when the cold water flowed over their hands. The Hawk gave me a crooked grin.

"I'll let you have a few cold beers but we've already split up the rest. You can have whatever's left over."

His laughter was coarse, he walked toward the fire and stirred the embers. Tony took a strong beer from the platform and opened it with his thumb. The foam sprayed across his hand. Then he turned around, looked me over then gave a little toss with his head, signaling for me to approach.

He handed me a beer. It was ice-cold. I opened it with my thumb just like he did, the foam tickled the back of my hand.

"What are we celebrating?"

He looked back out over the water, sucking the beer into him.

"My birthday."

I couldn't help but smile.

"Good. Because I have a surprise."

His eyes lit up. A hot glowing thread sliced through my body and I leaned over. As I was going to tell him about the car I caught sight of his neck. The skin had its usual pallor, his downy earlobe looked soft. But under his ear, like a shadow on the pale skin, was a bluish red mark.

I saw each broken blood vessel. He had leaned his head to the side for someone, someone had been allowed to fix their lips to his neck and bite, nibble, rub his skin until it broke. The glowing thread in my body cooled, it became a blunt piece of metal chafing against my heart. I no longer knew what to do with my hands. All the words disappeared and there was nothing I could do but put the beer can to my lips and drink. The Hawk's thick voice called for Tony, asking him to join him in the bunker so he could have a birthday present. I stayed put and took another beer from the pallet, trying in vain to push away the image of the mark on his neck.

IT WAS LONG after midnight. The party had
wound down, the shrieks and laughter had
softened into murmuring voices around the fire.

We sat on an outcrop a little ways away. The
Hawk had been circling Tony the whole night,
serving him, trying to entertain him with tough
commentary that Tony didn't even attempt to
smile at. But now the Hawk was passed out on
the bunker's cement floor, eyes half shut, snor-
ing deeply.

We sat there, Tony and me. The chill of the
bare rock worked its way through my jeans,
ahead of us the river's glinting water, behind us
the shadow of the forest, still and muted. The blu-
ish-red bite on his neck didn't bother me anymore because once again Tony had chosen me.
He'd sat with me by the fire, reached out his big
hand so that I could pull myself up, and said that

we were going to take a walk. As I stood up I came really close to him, my nose full of that musty dark smell that made me buzz and tingle as we went off on our own.

He drank most of his beer and handed me the dregs. As I drank he shoved me and the beer went down the wrong way. I coughed and spit and he laughed at me, it was a raspy laugh but not threatening, and when he asked for his present his voice was full of expectation:

"So, how about that surprise?"

I threw the empty beer can in a wide arc out into the water and got up, reaching my hand out so that he could stand up too.

"Come on."

And we walked out over the rocks, Tony followed me, ahead of us was the darkness and the forest and the car and I thought *It's happening, we're entering a state of wonder!*

Then somebody called his name.

A high-pitched voice, tinkling and enticing. It was one of the doe-girls. I recognized her from the night Tony had taken me to his shooting range. She was heading straight for us and waving drunkenly at Tony, her long slender arm flapping overhead. I wanted to reach out, I wanted to grab hold of Tony's jacket and pull him with me into the forest. Instead I paced, couldn't get a word out, shoved my hands into my jacket pockets and felt my heart pounding and pounding in my chest.

Tony watched the girl stumble around. Then he looked at me, his icy blue eyes glinted in the dark. He waved the doe-girl over.

There we were, on the outcrop, the girl and Tony and me. She was close to Tony, now and then her slender fingers touched his arm. We were only there a minute, before Tony nodded at the forest.

"Let's take a walk in the woods. Stretch our legs."

He glanced at the girl. Then at me. His eyebrows were raised, his mouth had the hint of a grin. I saw it. His intentions were clear, but I refused to acknowledge them. So I looked out over the water.

The drunk girl was pleading with her doe eyes. She eagerly took his hand and started walking. She thought he'd meant what he had said: there was a *we* between her and Tony.

When he noticed I wasn't following them, he glanced over his shoulder.

"You coming or what?"

His hand at the small of her back, her unsteady Bambi legs, her elegant, adorned hand feeling its way around his waist.

I shook my head.

He raised his chin, gave me a curious look from under his cap. In the darkness his eyes were like two metal buttons, they flashed. Maybe out of disappointment. He led the girl to the edge of the forest dragging her on when those wobbly high heels didn't want to carry her. I heard her sheepish laughter, the water seemed aflame.

Quietly I walked to the edge of the forest. Darkness clung to the trunks. Dry branches scratched my jacket like scrabbling spider legs. I stopped, listened to the rustling leaves and mumbling voices. But once my eyes had gotten used to the dark, I saw them.

Soft, rolling movements, his hand on her breast. Her hands around his neck. His body on top of hers. I had lain under that body, I remembered its weight and pulse.

I froze, transfixed by her movements.

How all of a sudden they changed.

She started trying to wriggle her way out from under his weight. These were panicked movements, going faster, getting jerkier. Her pale nails clawed at him, breaking against his jacket. Her legs twitched and kicked, her high heels tore holes in the earth and I heard her. First softly protesting, then her voice rose to a plea that broke into whimpering and tears.

For a second Tony's body stopped moving on top of her. I took a soundless step back, didn't want to be discovered. But he didn't turn around, didn't roll aside. He put his hand over her mouth, dug two fingers in between her lips and stifled her voice. She wheezed, fell silent. Her eyes were bright with fear, her nostrils quivered as she desperately tried get some air.

Tony's back in the darkness, his white buttocks lustrous above the waistband of his jeans and the terrified body under him, he was pushing himself into her without her consent and to think it was her and not me that he wanted to be inside of!

My legs felt mute but the adrenaline urged them on. I was a robot, I wasn't in control of my own movements. His body was clumsy, his radar was shut off, his vigilance dulled by greedy desire. I walked over to him and my head was a nest of snakes, a slithering black mass wriggling in front of my eyes. I couldn't stand what I was seeing, him taking what he wanted and using it up and throwing people away like they didn't matter. But they matter to me; Tony, *this matters to me and I'm not going to let you take anything else, never again.*

With all my might, I kicked.

My steel-capped toe hit his temple. He tumbled onto his back, away from the girl-body. I don't know what happened to her other than that she crawled out of the way. I didn't see her, I only saw Tony's vulnerable chest.

I kicked, kicked, kicked. Tony lay there on the ground and I saw his face and his surprise and his open fly, his dick sticking straight up, and I thought in a flash it was strange it hadn't gone limp. It just stood straight up and I drove the steel toe right into his balls and dick and all of it. Tony gasped. His body went limp, blood was running out of his mouth but his dick was still upright, mocking me. I kicked again and again. I heard voices but I didn't stop. I couldn't stop.

A scream cut through the air. A familiar sound, a voice I recognized. It had been a long time since I'd last heard it. He was clear as day as he came running: Momo's boy-face lit up between the branches. His mouth was twisted in desperation and his eyes, his eyes were dark and hot and wild as he pushed the branches aside and made his way to me, wordless and screaming like he'd lost his mind. The others from the party were behind him. They were craning their necks, wobbly on their feet, shouting to each other and pointing in confusion at the forest's edge.

I tripped, I slipped, I ran right into the woods. I dodged the thickest branches but the thin ones made my face bleed. Momo was behind me. He was shouting at me to stop, he tripped and fell and got up snorting. But I knew every root and hole in the ground because I had run here many times before and the sound behind me faded. In the end all I could hear was my own thundering pulse.

I don't remember when the forest ended. I don't remember how long I hid among the rusty containers. But the wisps of cloud skimming the sky, those I remember and the burning in my throat, my wheezing breath and whooshing lungs. The echo of the highway, the stiff iron necks of the harbor cranes. And that I finally crept out and and snuck over to the wharf. The rusty streaks on my hands as I dropped the boots over the edge and the cold moisture pushing its way through my socks. I stood there, looking at my feet. Two knobby, dirty-socked feet that seemed to be so far beneath me, as though my torso weren't connected to my legs.

BY THE TIME my neighborhood came into view, my socks were ragged. The cold had numbed my legs up to my knees, and I couldn't feel the pain or the wetness. My head was a hole, my thoughts were punctured blisters. I touched my cheeks—the wounds from the branches were like warpaint.

The neighborhood was quiet and still; not a sound could be heard as I coaxed opened Bella's gate. The greenhouse gleamed in the glow of the street lamps, and when I reached it I saw a large key in the padlock. I opened the flimsy glass door and climbed inside so I could see her.

The flower's head was hanging down to the cement floor. A number of dark purple petals had fallen off and landed in the gutter. Those still clinging to it were withered and brown at the tips. It was like she had cancer. I wanted to touch her, I longed to stroke her velvety head but she seemed so frail, like the slightest tremor could make her lose the rest of her petals. I didn't want to see her like this, it didn't want to see her bald and naked with her sensitive innards unprotected. I sighed, harder than I realized, and the breath reached her, shook her, and loosened yet another petal, which wafted into the gutter. It left a gash in her head. The pale yellow pollen had gone a stale brownish green.

I backed toward the door, slowly so as not to create any drag. Before I shut the door on her, I bowed my head and whispered quietly:

"They'll take care of you. Soon. You won't have to wait much longer."

I flushed what was left of my socks down the toilet, feeling only a hum in my feet as I rinsed them with hot water. The water turned brown with dirt and blood before whirling down the drain.

My body lay inside girl-pajamas in bed and stared at the light from the street on the ceiling. My limbs ached and pounded because of the bruises and swollen scratches and my feet burned and froze but deep inside, in my chest and in my head, there was basically nothing. I shut my eyes, wanted nothing, was nothing. Momo's roar floated in the folds of my brain. I saw him running through the woods, heard the snap of dry twigs.

I opened my eyes. It was the sound of glass breaking, a sharp tinkle. I shot up, stumbled to my lame feet and staggered to the window. Over in Bella's garden was a shadow. I limped to the door. I couldn't feel the doormat's rough bristles on my soles, I didn't feel the night-chilled flagstones or the hard gravel of the asphalt. I shouted but my voice didn't leave my throat. My body was slow like in a nightmare, but my eyes were wide open.

I could see him clearly.

Momo, a slim boy-shadow moving inside the glass walls. His arms jerked, made large splashing movements. Then he came out of the greenhouse, flicked open his lighter and turned to face me.

She caught fire. A blinding point expanding behind the glass wall, lapping higher and higher toward the ceiling.

I stood still. Something sliced through me.

Like a steel thread, a thin, sharp cut from the crown of my head to my arches.

I didn't have a mirror but I knew what was happening. It was a kind of death, exactly as I had imagined. He flowed out of me, right there on the asphalt, the boy-body shriveled and died. I was left alone with my girl-body. I peered at my hands. They were swollen and reddish, but they were two completely normal girl-hands being balled tight into fists then straightening back out. A thin stream of blood ran from my nose. I stuck my tongue out and tasted the dark, hot liquid. The townhouses jolted awake.

Rows of windows lit up, doors flew open, people rushed out in slippers and bathrobes and nightgowns. Somebody shouted for water, another said to call the fire department. The large panes of the greenhouse cracked one by one in the heat, thick black smoke rose from the roof. Momo was still on the garden path. Her boy-body was gone too, her girl-face flickered in the fire's glow. Her cheeks were sooty and streaked with tears, and when a man appeared and grabbed her by the arm she didn't resist.

I heard voices. Two people standing next to me. It took a while before I realized that they were my parents. Their voices came from an abyss, they repeated my name and shook me. I tore my eyes from the greenhouse. Someone grabbed me by the arm and led me away from the smoke and fire. When I put my foot on the rough doormat a cry rose to the sky, and when I turned my head I saw how they were holding Bella, how they were holding her tight to keep her from rushing into the flames.

MY PARENTS WHISPERED behind the walls.

A hot water bottle was at my feet in bed but I felt no heat. They took turns sitting with me, they rubbed my toes and my heels. I'm sure their hands were soft and kind but I couldn't feel them, it wasn't my skin they were touching. I remember snatches of conversation. "She's in shock," they said. "Get her a hot drink, let her be." They mumbled other things about the other two girls, about the rage that overcame the redhead when she'd seen what had happened. And the other one, she was in her parents' house crying and crying, refusing to say why she'd done it.

I was the third girl, and my eyes were glued to a fixed point all day.

WHEN NIGHT FELL my paralysis eased. I tiptoed out of bed and dressed warm. I left a note for my parents on my bed, saying I'd miss them but they shouldn't come looking for me. I put a few changes of clothing in a trunk. After that I pulled up the hood of my sweatshirt over my head and climbed out the window of my girlhood room for the last time.

In the moonlight I could see what was left of the greenhouse. I hadn't planned on going there but as I neared I heard scraping and panting. I opened the gate soundlessly, creeping over to get a better look.

It was Bella. She was kneeling among the broken glass, cracked pots, and charred gardening tools, digging frantically with a little spade through the ash, filtering the dust through her fingers. Then she swore, grabbed her hand, and lifted it in the moonlight to get a better look. That's when she saw me. I hesitated, stepped toward her but stopped, a few meters away.

"Did you cut yourself?"

She got up, brushing off her knees. It was just a gesture, her pants were caked with ash. Her arms were flecked with soot and her face was sort of expressionless, from sorrow or hate or maybe she didn't recognize my voice anymore, I didn't know which. Then she ran the back of her hand over her forehead, leaving a dark trail of soot.

"What do you want?"

I shrugged. She dropped to her knees again and kept digging. The wounded finger jutting out. Neither of us said anything at first. Then she said:

"Is it true, what Momo is saying?"

"What's she saying?"

"That you killed him."

I nudged a pot shard with the tip of my shoe, lobbed it into the bushes.

"I don't know. I think so. He wasn't moving."

Bella turned her unseeing gaze to the ash, her

lower lip trembled, and I wanted to add something, was searching for the words:

"There was a girl, he was hurting her, he . . ."

I couldn't say it out loud. The word was too difficult, too painful, too much for my mouth. I took another breath.

"Everything broke. Inside me. When I saw it."

Bella didn't reply. The words rang in my ears: *There was a girl, he was hurting her.*

I didn't know if the girl I was talking about was the one who'd been underneath him, or me.

Bella stopped digging. In the moonlight I could see that her cheeks were wet and streaked.

"So what are we supposed to do, do you think? Now that everything, there's nothing left, everything is ruined. For all three of us."

She grabbed at the ash, fistfuls of darkness ran through her fingers. Something in my chest burst. I wanted to throw my arms around Bella, return everything I'd taken from her. If I could've, I would've given her my life, or what was left of it. But all I could do was open my mouth, all I could offer her were a few meager words.

"I guess I should . . . go."

A moment passed. Then she nodded.

"Yeah, you should."

She went back to digging through her devastation. I walked toward the gate, feeling the trunk's weight on my shoulder and the pressure of tears behind my eyes, and with each step I wished she'd call after, tell me that there was another way out.

But Bella didn't say anything more. My last memory of her is of her fourteen-year-old girl-body kneeling in the ash and digging herself deeper and deeper into the remnants of the greenhouse.

AROUND THE BUNKER, it was deserted. The police lines were in the distance but I tried not to look over there. In the silence of night the creaking door sounded like a scream and I stopped, listening tensely for something over by the cordoned-off area. But I heard nothing—no voices, no barking. I went inside. The wine-red armchair stood watch in the barren room, the buttons in the upholstery tracked me with their gaze. I went up to it, put my hand to the cool leather, searched the cleft between the seat and the armrest. I didn't know where he kept the ammunition, but I knew it was loaded with at least one shot. With the gun in my hand I could see him sitting there, an uncannily clear image: the robber king on his throne. That rough thumb rubbing his chin, the bluish-green tattoo winding around his lower arm. And those eyes. Two steel-blue bullet holes that could only spark to life when close to death.

I turned the gun around in my hands, taking in the sleek lines in the tempered steel. When I looked up he was gone. The robber king's empty throne stared silently at me.

I stuffed the weapon inside the waistband of my jeans. Then I rinsed his headquarters of anything of value: credit cards, car keys, cash, skeleton keys, maps, knives. When the trunk was full, I left the steel door open to the elements.

I WAS ON the road for a while. Sleeping outside if it was warm, in the car if it was cold. On many nights I didn't sleep at all. I crouched in the chilled driver's seat and let the memories billow through my mind like smoke: Tony's moans, Momo's roar, Bella's silence. I caught my reflection in the car window and didn't want to recognize it, not wanting to acknowledge myself. I wasn't a girl, I'd gotten rid of her long ago. And the boy, him I'd crushed and consumed until only a monster remained.

I held my hands up in front of me as though they were mirrors, as though I could find a fresh, third face in my palms. But my hands offered no comfort.

MY MEMORIES OF those first months are few. Most everything is like a milky white fog, and every so often from the fog an island arises, a memory. I remember uninhabited summer cabins, tiptoeing through them, taking what I needed. Sometimes I stayed a while. Usually just for a few days, sometimes weeks. I never left a trace, and I was long gone before anyone returned.

Closer to cities I saw the black-and-white faces on the front pages. At first there were pictures of a boy, he was wanted for kicking another boy senseless. They didn't have a photograph. The face was an illustration, a phantom image with dark eyes sockets and a hardness to the mouth. I stared at him. The image grainy, features poorly rendered but in spite of everything: a face that had belonged to me.

Soon after came an image of the girl. The picture being used was almost a year old. The girl was a child, she was smiling and her eyes were open and innocent. She'd disappeared from her home under mysterious circumstances. They were searching for traces, a body, a clue but they found nothing. One of the newspapers ran a picture of her parents. They were sitting close together in the living room of a townhouse and their faces were veiled with worry. I touched their cheeks, I caressed their familiar features until my fingertips were gray with ink, but I didn't answer their pleas. It wasn't me they were missing. The daughter they wanted back no longer existed.

Certain memories are crystal clear.

A gravel road, a fence, an open gate. Old cars in a junkyard, a man in filthy overalls leaning over the hood of one. When I arrived, he just bent down closer to the cables. The road ended there. At first I was thinking about using his courtyard as a turning point but it had been a while since I'd spoken with anyone, and he seemed so calm and composed, the junkyard was a familiar chaos of tires and chassis and oil pans. I stopped, got out, asked if I could buy a can of gas. He raised his head, chewing slowly, and looked me over before breaking into a tobacco-stained grin.

"They looking for you?"

My voice was stuck. There was nothing I could say, all I did was shake my head. His grin widened.

"You sure as hell are wanted. You're a little hellraiser, boy, I've seen you in the papers."

My voice came back to me, forceful and firm:

"I am not a boy."

He sniffed, spit a brown loogie in the gravel and turned his back to me, waiting for me to leave. Then I went up to the hood of the car, stood in front of his bowed face, and unbuttoned my pants. He stood up straight, took a deep look at my groin.

We stood there for a moment, still. His eyes between my legs didn't bother me. My clothing covered my girl-body and my girl-body covered me, this had nothing to do with me, he could look until he got tired of it. His lips glinted and he took a step toward me. I pulled up my pants, tried to catch his eye, and it was only then, when our eyes met, that I felt naked. But I stood my ground. I could feel his tobacco breath on my face, I didn't back down. He chewed, scratched his neck with his thumbnail. Then he wiped his oily hands on a rag and said I could have fifteen liters for 200 kronor. I took the money out of my pocket once he went to fetch a can, I nodded in thanks. Then I turned the car around in the dusty gravel and drove away from the junkyard. I kept checking in the rearview mirror. The road was empty, he wasn't following me.

I didn't think he would find the car. It was in the forest at least five kilometers from his property, . but in the middle of the night I woke up because he was jimmying the lock open. I didn't see a car, he must've walked the whole way. He was panting and grabbing at my belt buckle. I searched underneath the seat, grabbed hold of the stiletto, flicked it open under his fleshy nose and he balked. Then I planted my foot to his chest and kicked. He tumbled backward but didn't leave, he stood up and started shouting. His voice was murky with booze. He shouted that I was a freak and that he'd turn me normal yet. I pushed the lock down, crawled over to the driver's seat, never taking my eyes off him. He staggered in front of the car with his fists on its hood. I started the engine, the rear wheels skidded in the dirt, and he hurled himself clumsily to one side, bellowing something I couldn't hear as I drove away.

THE NEXT NIGHT I broke into his compound. Several weeks of takings were stuffed into a coffee can in the filthy refrigerator, and I took them. I filled my trunk with gas and tools, winter tires, snow chains, spark plugs, batteries. Then I drove as far away from there as possible, and where the roads stopped was a house.

I arrived at twilight. It was an autumn day, sun glowing between the trees. The door was hanging open, one iron hinge had rusted away, several windows were broken, and the moss had climbed far up the decaying walls. I went in. The ceilings were low and the wallpaper was very old, large pieces had loosened and under them the walls were covered with yellowing newspaper. The furniture was covered with cloths, stiff and dark with grime. In the corner was a mirror caked with dust; my face looked frozen in the black-flecked glass. I touched my cheek. Bones jutted out from under the skin, the hair in matted tufts. She looked sort of dead, the creature in the mirror. Like she had died but happened to have gone on living by mistake. I turned the mirror to the wall, kept exploring the decaying house. Piles of leaves had blown in, and one of the rooms was covered in bird droppings, and in another some animals had made a bed of the moldering fabric scraps and trash. In the pantry birds and small animals had torn open the bags and ravaged most of what they contained, the leftovers were piled on the floor and shelves. I found some preserves, sharp beaks had made deep marks in the aluminum but I could still read what they contained. I'd never heard of the manufacturers, the cans must have been abandoned many years before. But there was a large fireplace and a wood-burning stove and an old telephone made of black Bakelite. I expected silence when I put the handpiece to my ear, but to my surprise there came a distant, buzzing tone. A forgotten sound, like the line should've been cut years ago but had stayed connected to the network by mistake. The tone wavered, as though it had just woken up, like it had been asleep for ages and was only now rising.

I stayed. Covered the windows with thick paper, fixed the hinge on the front door, cleared away the traces of birds and animals. I tried to get by as best I could with what I had, but every now and then I had to stock up on supplies. After the first autumn storm the paper windows weren't enough anymore and I hired a glazier who put in new panes. He got the last of my money for his troubles, thanking me happily as he thumbed the wad. I waited until his van had disappeared from sight before I threw my empty chest in the trunk of my car and set off to find replenishments. I never went far from the house, choosing roads where it was obvious that no one had driven for a long time. The car jolted over the gravel and pine cones and moss and often the road ended at an empty house.

Breaking into locked houses, walking through strange rooms and searching through other people's things should have put me ill at ease. But it wasn't like that. Empty rooms are like preserves of other people's lives. Once you step inside, the smell of cooking oil and spices, lavender sachets and perfume, bodies and cigarette smoke hits you like a second barrier. I could spend ages walking on their wooden floors, flipping through their books, reading their telephone notes, feeling the fabrics of their summer clothing tidily folded in chests of drawers. On the walls hung photographs of other people's families and children's drawings made for someone else, and in my imagination I made it mine. I nodded at the stern portraits, smiled at the childish watercolors, ran my finger over the scrawled signatures, and soon the children were running around me. I could hear their laughter, I saw their bare feet in the sun spots on the floor.

When darkness fell I took what was useful. Flour and grains and packets of cookies from the kitchen shelves, ointments and headache pills and soap wrapped in silk paper from the bathroom cabinet. My deft fingers ran over mattresses, sometimes finding hand-sewn seams, quick tight stitches like white scars in the fabric's pattern. I cut right through them, gutting the mattress like a fish, and took half of what was hidden in the stuffing. Then I covered it up neatly, on my way out I locked the doors and shut the bolts and ignored the rearview mirror as I drove off.

The next time my stocks were low I chose a different direction, finding other houses where I could live in other people's lives for a little while.

That's how time passed.

I froze and warmed up and froze again. The ground froze and thawed. A large tree fell on the house, cracking several roof tiles that I couldn't afford to replace. A spring downpour, the cellar flooding, me up to my knees in water, bailing. And the early summer day when I discovered that the bush by the southern wall was strewn with small pale-blue flowers. They'd bloomed overnight, burst out of their buds as if on command. I didn't know their name but I plucked two, pressed them in one of the old books in the house until they were dry and thin as silk paper. One I sent to the townhouse where my parents lived. The other I put in an unmarked envelope. I kept it next to my bed, every night before I fell asleep I saw the faded blank page staring back at me. That is, until one night a few months ago, when I wrote on it the name of the street where Bella's greenhouse had once been.

I'VE DRIVEN UP the map.

Through farmland and forest regions, past cities and fields and stark rocky coasts.

It's not far now.

Here the pines are windswept and stooped. My eyes ache, I have a cramp in my right foot, and my arms are falling asleep from having been stretched out so long. The roads on the map have gradually become more meandering, two cars barely have room to pass by each other, the edges of the asphalt are treacherously soft. In the twilight I almost drive past the old wooden sign. At the last second I see it, slam on the brakes, and yaw sharply onto the gravel road.

I drive into darkness. The large trees soak up the faint light from the sky, the old headlamps only manage to illuminate a few meters of darkness in front of me. The car lurches along the increasingly uneven surface. A tight grip on the wheel, eyes staring straight ahead, I see no light between the fir trees. Darker and darker it gets, the treetops seem to be bending toward me. I press down on the gas pedal, eager to find my way out of the mass of forest but the wheels skid and the car moves ever more slowly. Until I encounter a roadblock. It turns up around a bend, an unbending arm stretched across the road.

The engine stops. The headlamps cast white light across the roadblock, the lock, the fierce orange sign. My ears are ringing in the deep silence.

I don't want to ignore the unusual feeling at work in my chest. But I know. I still remember, if but distantly, how it feels to be afraid of the dark.

My jaw aches and when I open my mouth I realize how tense it is. I try not to let it bother me, I try to make my voice strong and sure when I say to myself out loud:

"So, I guess I'm walking."

Groaning, the car door opens. I sit in stillness, listening to the forest's sweeping silence before I set foot on the earth. Then, right by me comes a cry. The branches sway and a cold wind hits my face, the wild flapping of wings is all around as I dive back into the car, turning the key in the ignition again and again until the motor roars into action. Reason lurks in the back of my mind. "It was just a bird, you got scared by a bird," it says, but I can't listen. It's as though the darkness has finally streamed in through the gaps in the hull of the car and from there has made its way inside me, as though the bird's cry unleashed the dark fear I've been carrying with me for so long. I see their faces, Momo and Bella looking down from the canopy and suddenly I understand what they want. I'm on my way to a trial, at the end of the road my past is waiting to finally catch up with me, nipping at my heels, gnawing up my legs and swallowing me whole.

I can see all of this in front of me as I put the car in reverse, spin in the mud, and reverse the car along the treacherous surface. The flight instinct is built in, I know what it's like to turn and run, but what is like to stay?

Then, with a jerk, it stops. The earth sucks down the wheels and undercarriage, the engine sighs and gives up. The headlights gape into the night for a final second before going dark, the lights on the instrument panel shut off one by one right before my eyes. When I turn the key, the car doesn't even sputter, the key just turns round and round in the ignition.

It ends here, there is no way back.

Slowly I close my eyes, put one fist to my temple and reach the other under the seat. The shape is familiar but still foreign, I haven't touched it since I took it from Tony's headquarters. Now it's in my hand and I'm hearing his distant voice in my head.

Up and at an angle, toward the roof of your mouth. Then all you have to do is squeeze.

One squeeze, perhaps pain, after that nothing more.

For several long seconds I sit still, eyes squeezed shut to the dark.

Then I sense a movement outside. Gentle, like a flutter.

I open my eyes.

A wind has pulled in over the dome of the sky, the ragged clouds have been swept away and now the full moon is gleaming. Light floods the forest, and I can see clearly:

Swarms of butterflies on the windshield.

They are small, humble. Pale white wings with brownish-gray streaks, a fuzzy caterpillar body, and six delicate legs that cling to the window. Then they lift up like a single beast being consumed by the dark.

The slamming car door echoes in the forest. Now it's just me and the night and a soft shushing in the treetops. I turn on my flashlight. Darkness crowds beyond the reach of the pale beam and the forest smells like a cloth, wet and heavy on the nose, a savory scent of needles and moss and compost. All around is sighing and mumbling, but the butterflies are etched on my retina. Feet stumbling over holes and roots, more than a hundred steps until I see a light.

THE STORM LANTERN is hanging on a tree branch. This is where the butterflies have gone. They swarm around the bell, hurling their fuzzy bodies against the glass.

Hanging below the lantern is a cloth sack. By its opening, a piece of paper is pinned. The butterflies are crawling over the sack, scrabbling over the note on their way up toward the light. I tug the note free, turn it around and read a single word, printed in thick black charcoal.

Remember?

I stare at the word. Then I take the sack down, open it gingerly, and glimpse what's glittering in there. Clear starry night skies and silver threads come to mind, and I reach inside.

The memories explode in my head, they

whirl around each other, reproducing themselves as trembles in my fingers.

The Avian Conqueror is in the bag.

The fabric has paled but it's still shimmering, glittering gray like a crane's neck. The painted cardboard chest plate is broken here and there, a few of the rubber bands have stiffened and cracked but it still fits, following my body's shape when I slip it on.

I run my hands over the crooked pieces, feel a smile come sneaking from the very tips of my fingers.

At the bottom of the bag is the plaster mask. The silvery gray paint has flaked and the hooked beak has hooked even more. The plaster cracks and dust clouds when I try to bend the beak back in place. But when I pull the rubber band over my head, his face fits over mine and my eyes become his, and it's as though no time has passed at all.

I AM THE Avian Conqueror and I'm stalking through the forest.

Around me the butterflies flutter, following the light of my glittering feathered costume. My legs are stronger than tree trunks now, majestically I negotiate tree stumps and mossy tufts and come to the garden at the forest's edge.

Cracked garden furniture forms an arc in front of a small green-painted house. Around it burn tea lights and garden candles and torches, casting long shadows on the trees. On the rickety wooden table is the brown teapot, the cups, and the honeypot. The door to the house is open a crack. I listen for sounds inside but can't hear a thing, only the night wind buzzing through the treetops. I step onto the lawn and walk over to the table, taking off the teapot's top. Hot, spicy steam rises up, I pull the aroma deep into my lungs. And then I hear something from inside the house, rustling and giggling. I put the top back on the pot, clasp my hands behind my back, and feel my heart pounding under the armor.

Two shadows expand in the open doorway.

Ceremoniously, they step onto the stairs.

They are so beautiful.

They are so beautiful!

The Desert Creature's velvet tuxedo stretches over his chest. Several buttons are missing, the shirt is ripped and threadbare and worn sloppily. But the thick dark swell of hair is just as I remember it, it carpets his back. A crack running from the forehead to the chin has given the masked face an odd expression of concern; the nose and mouth are crooked.

Pierrot barely fits in his checkered costume. The button at the collar has been removed, leaving the lace at the collar free to wave under his chin. But the hat and mask look almost new, only the glossy rouge lacquer has darkened to a brownish black hue.

They are coming toward me, they are so close,

their hands reach for mine. Seams rip and clouds of dust billow from the plaster as we throw our arms around each other. My hooked nose cracks as I bury my face in the lace around Pierrot's neck. Their bodies are pressed tight to mine, their hands and breath envelop me.

What is a memory, what is it made of? How sparkling clear and alive, how saturating must a memory be for it to be called reality? My ears remember, my lungs, fingers, and lips remember. I'm still carrying the child inside me, and it has been roused. Curious, it draws the night forest into its lungs, reaches out its stiff silver-clad limbs, and peers at its playmates through the plaster mask.

We play for hours, the Desert Creature, Pierrot, and me. We play in the torchlight, raise toasts, laugh, and talk over each other. We remember the dances and we dance them, we remember the songs and we bellow them, so loud and off-key that owls blink in the trees, affronted. Night thickens, the moon moves across the sky but we never want to stop, this can never end, we'll never have our fill of the game or of each other. The Desert Creature walks on his hands across the lawn and Pierrot and I dance the medicine man's dance around him. We stomp and buck on the earth until our feet are black. Behind the cardboard armor my heart swells, fills to the brim with joy.

Finally we fall in a heap on the grass. The torches have gone out; it's probably cold but we don't notice, we lie close together in a pile. Bella's head is once again resting on my chest and Momo's legs are tangled in mine. We've played our costumes to pieces, they're hanging in tatters from our arms and legs. We've thrown our masks into the grass and around us is the smell of play and sweat, it rises like steam from our bodies and mixes with the cold.

The moon has sunk into the treetops. A lone butterfly sits on my arm, silently snapping its pale wings open and shut, as though asleep. Bella's breath moves through my body, heavy and slow. In sleep she turns her head and nuzzles the hollow of my neck. Momo's arms are spread wide on the grass. Her mouth is open and from her throat rises a gentle snore. I smile. My eyelids are very heavy, I let them drop, prepared to be taken by sleep.

And then I feel a movement, an ever so slight tickle, when the butterfly lifts up from my arm.

Slowly, I turn my head, follow its path as it flies toward one of the house windows. A soft shimmer is coming from the inside. The butterfly thuds against the window pane, hurling its body at the cold light again and again.

Like a snake I wriggle out of the nest of bodies and then tiptoe as quietly as I can so as not to wake the others. The Avian Conqueror's seams have burst; he falls off of me as I traverse the lawn, leaving a trail of painted cardboard and dirty rags behind and leaving me naked.

The house is small, a kitchen and two rooms. In one is a bed, the other is covered with bookcases from floor to ceiling. Along one wall are large earth-filled pots, by the other is an armchair with a blanket and a reading lamp. The desk is loaded with open books. I catch sight of the colorful illustrations and I want to enter, I want to read what Bella has read about and see what she is growing in the pots, but when I pass through the doorway a mirror confronts me.

It is leaning against the wall, large enough to reflect a fully grown person. The frame is wide and ornamental and the gilding has flaked, here and there large splinters have fallen off the wood. But the glass is spotless. I see myself clearly.

Long arms, rough hands. A body with almost no subcutaneous fat, muscles like knots under my skin. The chest is almost completely flat, nipples dark and stiff with cold. The skin dips behind the collar bones and from them rises the neck, with blue pulsing veins.

As though my body still holds the memory of the boy, as though the emergence of the woman has broken down, stopped. There is a boy in the reflection and he is gaunt, not fully developed, childishly hairless. The woman falls like a veil over him, protecting him with her shell.

It is a person.

I caress my body, feeling my skin against my fingers and my fingers against my skin. I put my palm to the mirror's palm, press my forehead to the mirror's forehead, look deep into my own eyes. An adult gaze flashes, but it isn't dead anymore, it's no longer feeble and sad. No, my eyes are twinkling with life.

I smile at it.

It smiles back.

IT's ALREADY LIGHT when I wake up.

I'm sitting in the armchair wrapped in a blanket. The front door is ajar. Birds are twittering in the garden and someone is humming a song. Quietly I get up, the blanket clutched around my body, and tiptoe across the uneven floorboards. Momo is in the large bed in the bedroom, her hand is under her cheek, and the Desert Creature's mask is hung around her neck like a hunting trophy. I stroke her forehead with my finger. Still asleep, she smiles a little and sighs.

I start looking for my clothes, then remember that I left them by the storm lantern; they're soaking wet with dew and moss. On the floor are a pair of green overalls and a yellow shirt, way too big. I put them on and smile at how the fabric swallows my spindly body.

"You're awake. Good."

I turn around. It's Bella. She's wearing overalls and a shirt, too, but her body fills out the garments just right. Her breasts swell behind the snaps on the suspenders, her cheeks have a red glow. Around her fuzzy hair a cloud of butterflies flutters. They crawl along her legs and arms, clustering on her extended hand.

"Come on. She's waiting for us."

FIN

JESSICA SCHIEFAUER has established herself as one of Sweden's foremost writers of literary young adult fiction. Her widely praised first novel, *If You Were Me* (2009), was followed by the August Prize-winning *Pojkarna* (2011, published  in English as *Girls Lost*), which has been translated into several languages. *Girls Lost* was also nominated for the Nordic Council Debut Children's Book Award. In addition to two theater adaptations of the the novel, a film based on the book, *Girls Lost* (2016), was a huge critical success and won several international awards. Schiefauer's third novel, *The Eyes of the Lake* (2015), also won the August Prize, thus cementing her position on the Sweden literary scene. Exploring questions of self-esteem, coming of age, sexuality, and gender, Schiefauer engages adults as well as young adult readers. She lives in Gothenburg, Sweden.

SASKIA VOGEL is from Los Angeles and lives in Berlin, where she works as a writer and Swedish-to-English literary translator. She has written on the themes of gender, power, and sexuality for publications such as *Granta*, *The White Review*, *The Offing*, and *The Quietus*. Her translations include work by such leading female authors as Lina Wolff, Johannes Anyuru, Karolina Ramqvist, and Rut Hillarp. Previously, she worked in London as *Granta Magazine*'s global publicist and in Los Angeles as an editor at the AVN Media Network, where she reported on the business of sex work and adult pleasure products. Her debut novel, *Permission*, was published in 2019 and has been translated into several languages.

Thank you all
for your support.
We do this for you,
and could not do
it without you.

DEEP
VELLUM

PARTNERS

FIRST EDITION MEMBERSHIP
Anonymous (9)
Donna Wilhelm

TRANSLATOR'S CIRCLE
Ben & Sharon Fountain
Meriwether Evans

PRINTER'S PRESS MEMBERSHIP
Allred Capital Management
Robert Appel
Charles Dee Mitchell
Cullen Schaar
David Tomlinson & Kathryn Berry
Jeff Leuschel
Judy Pollock
Loretta Siciliano
Lori Feathers
Mary Ann Thompson-Frenk & Joshua Frenk
Matthew Rittmayer
Nick Storch
Pixel and Texel
Social Venture Partners Dallas
Stephen Bullock

AUTHOR'S LEAGUE
Christie Tull
Farley Houston
Jacob Seifring
Lissa Dunlay
Stephen Bullock
Steven Kornajcik
Thomas DiPiero

PUBLISHER'S LEAGUE
Adam Rekerdres
Christie Tull
Justin Childress
Kay Cattarulla
KMGMT
Olga Kislova

EDITOR'S LEAGUE
Amrit Dhir
Brandon Kennedy
Dallas Sonnier
Garth Hallberg
Greg McConeghy
Linda Nell Evans
Mary Moore Grimaldi
Mike Kaminsky
Patricia Storace
Ryan Todd
Steven Harding
Suejean Kim
Symphonic Source
Wendy Belcher

READER'S LEAGUE
Caitlin Baker
Caroline Casey
Carolyn Mulligan
Chilton Thomson
Cody Cosmic & Jeremy Hays
Jeff Waxman
Joseph Milazzo
Kayla Finstein
Kelly Britson
Kelly & Corby Baxter
Marian Schwartz & Reid Minot
Marlo D. Cruz Pagan
Maryam Baig
Peggy Carr
Susan Ernst

ADDITIONAL DONORS
Alan Shockley
Amanda & Bjorn Beer
Andrew Yorke
Anonymous (10)
Anthony Messenger
Ashley Milne Shadoin
Bob & Katherine Penn
Brandon Childress
Charley Mitcherson
Charley Rejsek
Cheryl Thompson
Chloe Pak
Cone Johnson
CS Maynard
Daniel J. Hale
Daniela Hurezanu
Dori Boone-Costantino
Ed Nawotka
Elizabeth Gillette
Erin Kubatzky
Ester & Matt Harrison
Grace Kenney
Hillary Richards
JJ Italiano
Jeremy Hughes
John Darnielle
Julie Janicke Muhsmann
Kelly Falconer
Laura Thomson
Lea Courington
Leigh Ann Pike
Lowell Frye
Maaza Mengiste
Mark Haber
Mary Cline
Maynard Thomson
Michael Reklis
Mike Soto

pixel ||| texel

ADDITIONAL DONORS, CONT'D

Mokhtar Ramadan
Nikki & Dennis Gibson
Patrick Kukucka
Patrick Kutcher
Rev. Elizabeth & Neil Moseley
Richard Meyer
Scott & Katy Nimmons
Sherry Perry

Sydneyann Binion
Stephen Harding
Stephen Williamson
Susan Carp
Susan Ernst
Theater Jones
Tim Perttula
Tony Thomson

SUBSCRIBERS

Audrey Golosky
Ben Nichols
Brittany Johnson
Caroline West
Chana Porter
Charles Dee Mitchell
Charlie Wilcox
Chris Mullikin
Chris Sweet
Courtney Sheedy
Damon Copeland
Derek Maine
Devin McComas
Francisco Fiallo
Fred Griffin
Hillary Richards

Jody Sims
Joe Milazzo
John Winkelman
Lance Stack
Lesley Conzelman
Martha Gifford
Michael Binkley
Michael Elliott
Michael Lighty
Neal Chuang
Radhika
Ryan Todd
Shelby Vincent
Stephanie Barr
William Pate

FORTHCOMING FROM DEEP VELLUM

AMANG · *Raised by Wolves*
translated by Steve Bradbury · TAIWAN

MARIO BELLATIN · *Mrs. Murakami's Garden*
translated by Heather Cleary · MEXICO

MAGDA CARNECI · *FEM*
translated by Sean Cotter · ROMANIA

MIRCEA CĂRTĂRESCU · *Solenoid*
translated by Sean Cotter · ROMANIA

MATHILDE CLARK · *Lone Star*
translated by Martin Aitken · DENMARK

PETER DIMOCK · *Daybook from Sheep Meadow* · USA

LEYLÂ ERBIL · *A Strange Woman*
translated by Nermin Menemencioğlu · TURKEY

FERNANDA GARCIA LAU · *Out of the Cage*
translated by Will Vanderhyden · ARGENTINA

ANNE GARRÉTA · *In/concrete*
translated by Emma Ramadan · FRANCE

GOETHE · *Faust*
translated by Zsuzsanna Ozsváth and Frederick Turner · GERMANY

PERGENTINO JOSÉ · *Red Ants: Stories*
translated by Tom Bunstead and the author · MEXICO

FOWZIA KARIMI · *Above Us the Milky Way: An Illuminated Alphabet* · USA

TAISIA KITAISKAIA · *The Nightgown & Other Poems* · USA

DMITRY LIPSKEROV · *The Tool and the Butterflies*
translated by Reilly Costigan-Humes & Isaac Stackhouse Wheeler · RUSSIA

JUNG YOUNG MOON · *Arriving in a Thick Fog*
translated by Mah Eunji and Jeffrey Karvonen · SOUTH KOREA

GORAN PETROVIĆ · *At the Lucky Hand, aka The Sixty-Nine Drawers*
translated by Peter Agnone · SERBIA

C.F. RAMUZ · *Jean-Luc Persecuted*
translated by Olivia Baes · SWITZERLAND

ETHAN RUTHERFORD · *Farthest South & Other Stories* · USA

TATIANA RYCKMAN · *The Ancestry of Objects* · USA

MIKE SOTO · *A Grave Is Given Supper: Poems* · USA

MUSTAFA STITOU · *Two Half Faces*
translated by David Colmer · NETHERLANDS